STOOPID

Ed & Bo
Get Wooed

MISADVENTURE #2

Laura McGehee

EPIC
Press

Ed & Bo Get Wooed
Stoopid: Book #2

Written by Laura McGehee

Copyright © 2016 by Abdo Consulting Group, Inc.

Published by EPIC Press™
PO Box 398166
Minneapolis, MN 55439

Cover design by Dorothy Toth
Images for cover art obtained from iStockPhoto.com
Edited by Ryan Hume

LIBRARY OF CONGRESS CATALOGING-IN-PUBLICATION DATA

McGehee, Laura.
Ed & Bo get wooed / Laura McGehee.
p. cm. — (Stoopid ; #2)
Summary: Ed & Bo are two recently graduated stoners with a growing business and
an even faster growing reputation. When they are flown out to Silicon Valley by a
'shady' potential investor, they must wade through incredible meals, flashy accom-
modations, unorthodox work habits, and a hell of a lot of snack food to determine
just how far they are willing to go for their future.
ISBN 978-1-68076-058-3 (hardcover)
1. High schools—Fiction. 2. High school seniors—Fiction. 3. Interpersonal
relations—Fiction. 4. Friendship—Fiction. 5. Graduation (School)—Fiction.
6. Young adult fiction. I. Title.
[Fic]—dc23
2015903980

EPICPRESS.COM

To Andrew, for letting me write this on his computer as we drove across the country, even when the radio didn't work

1

"So that's essentially how it went," Bo proclaimed as he took a bite of cherry pie. Ed sat at the opposite end of their favorite couch, stress-eating pie by the mouthful. "The government realized JFK was a problem and so they took him out. This lone gunman bullshit doesn't make sense if you look at the shot patterns."

"I learned a long time ago to never trust any of your theories," Ed responded. "I have never seen any conclusive evidence that Belfroy is a robot."

"That's because you're living your life with your eyes closed, Ed!" Bo shouted, cherry pie spilling out of his mouth ever so slightly. He licked his lips to retrieve the lost crumbs, letting the crunchy cinnamon crust rest on his tongue for just a moment. Ed refused to respond and continued to eat cherry pie far faster than seemed safe. He shoveled bite after bite into his mouth, not at all savoring every crumb but instead forcing the tart cherry and sweet, flaky crust to leave mere remnants of flavor as it went down only partially chewed. He preferred flavor by force, and besides, he got to eat more pie that way.

The boys were in their element, seated comfortably in Ed's garage. Remnants of old joints littered the makeshift tin-can ashtray next to Ed's feet. The DinoBong majestically rested as if on display on a table in the center of the room. A few last tendrils of smoke floated up from the bong, joining the smoke-filled garage. The tacked-up posters of concerts, supermodels, and weird skateboarding designs suggested it was a boys' hang out place, but the large steel shelving unit filled with labeled bins and items suggested something else, something more adult. An expansive whiteboard stood in front of the shelves, filled with what appeared to be gibberish, but upon further examination, depicted an intricate flow chart delivery system. "Bo" and "Ed" each had arrows pointing to different neighborhood areas with codes that corresponded to codes on the shelving units. There were also several newly added names—Terry, Alexandra, and Mitchell. It was the central control whiteboard, but at the moment, it was just a backdrop to Ed and Bo's bickering.

"If Belfroy is a robot, why would he be a high school guidance counselor?" Ed asked skeptically.

"So he can recruit the youth to be a part of his evil robot plan to dismantle humanity! How many times do I have to say it?" Bo shouted back.

Ed and Bo argued more often than not arguing, but they always managed to resolve it over a shared meal, a shared joke, or a shared joint. This time it was all three. Ed rolled a new joint in twenty-eight seconds flat, a new record, and offered it to Bo to light up. Bo could never stay mad at Ed when Ed offered him weed.

"Albert is looking pretty fat these days, man," Bo said with a wry smile. "You might even call him Fat Albert," he finished triumphantly. Ed groaned but had to chuckle in spite of himself.

"That one is getting really old, dude," he said sternly, although once a smile started he couldn't stop it. "I'm also not exactly sure who the original Fat Albert is."

The real Albert meowed angrily in the corner of the garage and both boys laughed loudly. It wasn't the first time Ed had thought that maybe his cat understood English, and it probably would not be the last. Bo reached for his lighter and ignited the tightly-packed joint. A wider smile spread across his face, which grew even wider after the second and third hit, and by the time he passed the joint back to Ed he was grinning. Ed soon joined him in width of smile as the warmth of weed flowed through him.

They both ate another piece of cherry pie that seemed to taste fuller, richer, and more complex than before. The tart cherries divvied up into layers of flavor, each more surprising than the last. The sourness of the initial bite gave way to tangy, sweet, and soft remnants. Ed and Bo finished their respective pieces of pie with the speed of several joints worth of weed, and Ed posed a very important question.

"Do you think that JFK or Obama had better sex?"

Bo considered for many tortured minutes of indecision. He thought about the scandalous Marilyn Monroe relationship with JFK, but also the obvious love shared between Michelle and Barack. This was one of the harder questions he'd ever had to answer.

"JFK." He finally answered. "Not with his wife, but with the other ladies. He probably had terrible sex with his wife."

"But Barack and Michelle—" Ed started to protest.

"I know, I know, they share a very apparent

trust and love. But that guy has gotten so *old* during office, there's no way he's doing cool sex things anymore."

"Cool sex things . . . like what?" Ed asked.

"Um . . . " Bo trailed off. His sexual exploits had taken place entirely at Camp Tuckabahtchee in a dark bunk bed on the last night of summer camp two years ago. He was certainly not qualified to give any opinion on cool sex, but somehow those three clumsy minutes in the cabin gave him a world of knowledge over Ed. Ed's unfortunately thin frame, incredibly pale skin, need to wear glasses, and inability to converse with women had left him a high school graduate who had yet to do the deed. He had to sit back and watch the kids at Interius Montgomery High discuss who had sex with whom and pretend he couldn't hear when people asked him about his conquests. Sometimes he really couldn't hear, because his ears were not very strong.

"Probably the kinda stuff they do in porn," Bo

decided. "Like weird positions and things and a lot of showers. Girls seem to really like that." Ed nodded in agreement, because in a sexless world, all he knew was from porn. He assumed that his first time would probably be the result of a delivery that made the customer *very* happy, and that was only part of the motivation for running Square One. The other part of the motivation was the hope that the fateful delivery would be made to Hayley Plotinsky, his most recent "one" that he hoped to lose his virginity to. He didn't exactly know what she was like or what she was into or how to talk to her, but he did know that she had long black hair and eyes that seemed to sparkle in the sunlight but also without sunlight. That was all he needed to know.

Ed and Bo had recently become semi-famous quasi-celebrities in the aftermath of graduation at Portland's Interius Montgomery High School. Under threat of being held back their senior year, Ed and Bo had created and somewhat successfully ran Square One, a service that connected customers with the answer to the simple question: "What do you want?" Although they hadn't won the Young Rising Entrepreneur Competition, they had gained the attention of the eerily handsome Paolo Müllers, a young business star himself. With his guidance, they had spent the end of their year expanding the business and making it slightly more legit. They learned about spreadsheets and business stuff like that. They even hired other people to be a part of the delivery team. Their shelves were made of steel and equipped with labels now—this was the big leagues.

Graduation had come and gone much as could be expected, but as word spread about Square One, Ed and Bo became busier and busier. They had been on summer vacation for a few weeks now, and had started to forget that they ever had to go to school in the first place. Each and every day, they smoked, they ate, and they delivered, usually in that order. Sure, they didn't really have plans for what to do next, but just going with the flow seemed to be a plan enough. They didn't really have time to think about how they weren't going to college in the fall like their friends or that if this business didn't work out, they'd have to get stupid jobs at Applebee's. For now, they were their own bosses, and they were kind of good at it.

Though you most certainly would not have been able to see any of this by just looking at the young idiots. Ed wore a gray t-shirt emblazoned with the words, "No I will not fix your computer." It was incredibly stained from meals prior but also more recently stained with cherry pie. It gave Ed the overall look of someone who got dressed in the dark, because he did. Bo had grown his hair out to the point of needing to tie it back into a ponytail, which imbibed him with the aura of a displaced hippie. But as soon as he opened his mouth to discuss his bizarre conspiracy views, like the Eiffel Tower actually being a radio tower built by the French to communicate with other galaxies, he became much less of a hippie and much more of a crazed lunatic.

Ed scraped the bottom of the pie tin, searching for leftover crumbs or a drop of cherry pie juice. He licked his fork clean, and Bo did the same. The first course of the night had been ravaged, but there was still courses two through ten, depending on how many bags of salt and vinegar chips they ate that night. The two boys sank deeper into the couch as the salt and vinegar chips savagely ripped away the sugar coating and left in its place the dry bitter vinegar bite that they both couldn't stay away from. They munched and continued to discuss the future of their business.

"You're so right. A manta ray would be the perfect girlfriend," Bo said and Ed nodded in agreement.

"She'd be all, 'Oh, Bo, let me cover you with my wide body and protect you from sharks,'" Ed said in a high-pitched female manta ray voice.

"Then she'd be like 'Ed, would you like to have

dinner tonight? I made algae!'" Bo continued. They broke out into laughter, the JFK conspiracy debate far in the past.

"Dude. We totally need to start offering a manta ray girlfriend to our customers," Ed declared, which just made both of them laugh even harder.

"Now, would this item be a literal or a metaphorical addition to your inventory?" asked a voice from the corner of the room. The boys both jumped and turned to see none other than Paolo Müllers sitting in the old beanbag chair, a green notepad in one hand and a pen in the other. He wore a charming gray-black suit that looked as soft as Albert, although he avoided any and all contact with the cat due to the potential for hair contamination.

"Dude!" Bo exclaimed.

"How long have you been here?" Ed added.

Paolo looked between the two of them as if they were an unsolvable puzzle. "For a very long time. I brought you the pie? We were talking about your favorite foods?"

"Did we tell you about—" Bo began with excitement.

"Salt and vinegar chips? Yes, for thirty minutes," Paolo said without expression. "And also about pizza rolls, soda, Chinese food, peanut butter products, all candy . . . " Paolo continued to name food product after food product and Ed and Bo couldn't help but giggle. Their favorite foods had never been compiled in a list like this, and it was pretty impressive.

"—And 'things that shouldn't go well together but do,'" Paolo finished breathlessly. "Did I miss anything?"

Ed and Bo shook their heads, both grinning. For the first time, a thought struck Bo, something he had never exactly considered.

"Why do you need to know that?" Bo asked. Ed nodded, intrigued—he had never really questioned the fact that Paolo had been spending inordinate amounts of time just watching them, asking a lot of questions, and writing down everything they said.

"Oh, just getting to know you," Paolo said offhandedly. The boys couldn't investigate any further, because at that moment, the garage door opened with a startling bump. Natalie and Ms. DeLancey wearily walked up the driveway, equipped with suitcases and sunhats and fresh off their mother-daughter cruise that Ed had firmly declined to attend.

"Yo, boners, you missed out on some kickass cruising," Natalie declared as she wheeled her luggage in. Her normally pale face was now bizarrely tanned, save for a wide sunglass mark around her eyes. She looked like a raccoon, specifically one who wore sunglasses.

"Natalie! Don't use that kind of language in front of our guest!" Ed retorted before Ms. DeLancey could.

"Don't tell me how to talk—" Natalie began furiously, but trailed off when she turned and made eye contact with Paolo's steel-gray eyes. They were the kind of eyes that perpetually stopped people in their tracks.

"Oh! A guest!" Ms. DeLancey sputtered, fumbling with her suitcase and equally stopped in her tracks. Paolo jumped up and smoothly crossed the garage to take the baggage from both Natalie and Ms. DeLancey. They stood and silently gaped, making both Ed and Bo a little nervous.

"Hello. It's a pleasure to finally meet you two. I've heard so much about you, but honestly, it doesn't live up to seeing you in person," Paolo said with a confident glimmer in his eyes. Both women flushed and murmured "hellos" back.

"Make yourself at home," Ms. DeLancey muttered under her breath. "Did you offer him any pizza rolls, Ed?"

"Yes, Mom," Ed said flatly, a little confused at the way his mother and sister exchanged looks with Paolo. Bo sat next to him, equally confused and bristling a bit, but for the entirely different reason of being hopelessly in love with his best friend's sister. Paolo continued to smile dashingly, somehow making eye contact with both Ms. DeLancey and Natalie at the same time. They both looked as if they had just seen a ghost—an incredibly handsome one, at that. He took the bags inside and the women followed in a daze, leaving the two boys alone on the couch.

The boys sat in silence, each struggling to figure out what they felt. All they could tell was that there was a very strange mixture of displeasure and jealousy. They didn't have any chance to put the combative mixture into words, because before long, Paolo was back in the garage, smiling his smile that even made Ed and Bo get lost a little. When Paolo gracefully sat back down into the beanbag chair—a feat that is by no means easy—and handed them a joint wrapped in white paper with a gold trim, bearing the emblem "COTLAW," Ed and Bo had firmly forgotten all about the question of why Paolo was there.

"Well, that was a great business development meeting. I really think we got a lot covered," Paolo said with a smile.

"Yeah. Us too," Ed said, looking at Bo like he'd forgotten to do his homework and gotten away with it.

"You boys have all your flight information, right?" Paolo asked. Ed and Bo darted looks at each other. They felt the lies fall out of their mouth and saw the dawning of Terror Town in the metaphorical distance, the marker of their smoking anxiety.

"Of course!" Ed said.

"Totally," Bo agreed.

Paolo nodded, a grin spreading across his face. "This trip will change your lives. I can't wait. Anyways, I'll see you guys tomorrow. Make loads of money tonight," he yelled back over his shoulder as he left through the garage door. As soon as he left, Ed and Bo turned to each other in a full-fledged panic.

"We can't keep doing this!" Ed said.

"Well, I don't see how we can ask him *now* where we're going and what we're doing when it's been three weeks!" Bo shouted back. They remembered that Paolo had told them something about a big trip long ago, but had not been able to remember any other detail at all. A few weeks of continued lying meant that now the boys were going somewhere at some time and had no idea of the details. Ed looked over at Bo and noticed his thinking face, which was exactly the same as his pooping face. But since Bo was not on the toilet at the moment, he knew there could only be one explanation. "You're thinking, aren't you? That's totally your thinking face. Come on. Spill it. What's on your mind, dude."

"Nothing."

"I don't believe you."

"Nothing!"

"Tell me or I'll eat the last piece of pie," Ed said with his fork hovering threateningly over the sole remaining slice.

"All right! I just . . . am not exactly sure if I trust Paolo," Bo said cautiously, watching Ed's face as he spoke.

"Oh. That's it?" Ed asked with a laugh.

"Just, like, he's been asking us all these personal questions for weeks now, and I'm not really sure how that applies to business."

"Yeah. I mean the dude is really strange, but it's probably because he's foreign or whatever," Ed said offhandedly.

"What? He's American."

"I'm pretty sure he's from Switzerland."

"You made that up."

"Yeah, he might be from the Netherlands," Ed said nonchalantly, and then threw a tiny remaining piece of pie at Bo. Despite his worrying, Bo leapt into the air and caught it squarely in his mouth.

"Stop worrying. You worry too much. Enjoy the free pie and the free weed while we are still young enough to enjoy it," Ed said, uncharacteristically calm. He was usually the one to feel the rising anxiety of imminent danger, but with Paolo, he only felt the rising anxiety of repeated lying. Paolo seemed like the big brother or young uncle he had never had, and maybe he wasn't even all that upset that his Mom had reacted that way when she met him. It was kind of nice to know an older guy that wasn't the mailman or Albert the cat. In fact, he didn't even mind all that much that he didn't know where he was going on the imminent trip, because at least Paolo was taking him.

Bo chewed his cherry pie, reveling in the flavors of fresh cherries and recently toasted dough for the last time before swallowing with finality. All he knew was that Paolo had an effect on Natalie that Bo had never even dreamed of having, because even in his dreams, Natalie still mostly just made fun of him. Maybe there was something to the whole mysterious, confident, charming thing Paolo had going on.

"Alright. I'm still hungry," Bo said as he looked at the empty pie box before them, and then over to the corner where a stack of six empty pie boxes remained.

"Paolo sure loves pie," Bo remarked. "Or, I guess, we do." When Ed didn't respond, he looked to see him intently struggling to light the DinoBong.

"No, man, you gotta light and inhale *before* you push down," Bo said.

"Don't tell me how to smoke my own Velocidactyl," Ed responded, pointing to the emblazoned name on the left side: "Ed."

"It's half mine, too," Bo reminded him, pointing to the other side that bore his name. Bo's birthday present to Ed had really been an investment in the future of Square One. Some of their most intelligent business decisions, like getting dragon-adorned uniforms and hiring the sixth grade cycling star Terry as a delivery girl, had come about after the good ol' DinoBong. Ed succeeded in the correct pushing to pulling ratio and took a hit that was probably the size of a dinosaur, a baby one at the very least. He coughed for several minutes and passed the DinoBong to Bo, who procured an equally large hit on his first try. He was much more of a bong man than Ed, who loved the personalization of joints. But at the end of the day, they really just enjoyed smoking together.

2

"**I am so glad we are here,**" **Bo whispered** to Ed across the booth while fixating on his favorite picture of a flower growing between two mossy rocks. They had returned to Al's Diner, the greasy go-to place for special occasions. Usually they reserved the diner for times of strife, but tonight, they were just really, really high. Ed hid behind his menu and surveyed the people around him, fully aware that Hayley Plotinsky worked at Al's Diner. The town was aflutter with speculation about Summer Slam, the town's annual send-off for the senior class. It was in a week or two or three or something—Ed and Bo could never really keep track. Mostly, they just cared about food.

"Chili bacon cheese fries? Ew," Natalie declared, sitting across from Ed and Bo. Ms. DeLancey had announced that she had a very important phone conference and therefore couldn't make dinner, so Natalie had to go out with her big brother. Neither Ed nor Natalie questioned that Ms. DeLancey had a phone conference when she hadn't exactly had a job in the past few years; they were both preoccupied with the upsetting fact that they had to eat together in public.

"Natalie's a vegetarian now," Ed said with visible disgust. Bo nodded politely, thinking that it was pretty cool to have such strong morals, but also thinking that chili bacon cheese fries sounded pretty amazing right now.

"That's pretty cool to have such strong morals," Bo said, eyes shifting away from that beautiful purple flower picture on the wall and focusing on the one in Natalie's hair.

"Thank you, Bo. You understand me," she said lightly, still searching through the menu. Bo's heart fluttered briefly, and then pounded through his chest when Ed screamed and pointed across the room. Bo and Natalie both turned quickly to see two mice chasing each other across the linoleum floor.

"You really need to get over your mouse phobia," Natalie said flatly.

"For the last time, Natalie, it's not a phobia, mice are just objectively disgusting!" Ed insisted. He looked to Bo for support, but Bo just shrugged.

"It's only Ham and Cheese," Bo said. "No need to be afraid."

"You named them?" Natalie asked incredulously. Bo shrugged sheepishly, and Natalie smiled. "That's actually pretty cool."

Bo's heart was fluttering again, so quickly that it alarmed him. It may have been the weed, or perhaps hormones, or maybe even true love, but it all felt a lot like a heart attack. But then he saw Natalie's eyes focus on someone past him, and twisted around in his seat to see Cameron Walcot smiling back. Now his heart very literally dropped to the bottom of his feet. Ed noticed none of this, distracted again in his own fantasy of Hayley pulling him into the back, taking her clothes off and then taking his clothes off and so forth. He gazed dreamily into the grimy kitchen, thinking that he wouldn't even care that he would probably get grease all over his clothes, and maybe burn his bare body on some splashing oil. It would so totally be worth it, as long as those mice didn't run by again.

Natalie snapped them all out of their revelry when she stood up abruptly. "You guys are getting quiet and weird again. Order me a veggie burger, please." With that, she was gone. Ed and Bo both twisted to watch her make her way over to Cameron's table and hug him warmly. The hug lasted too long for either of their tastes.

"Since when are they friends?" Bo asked, struggling to mask the panic in his voice and trying very hard to avoid a visit to Terror Town.

"Um. I think my Mom mentioned that the Walcots were on the cruise as well," Ed said, also staring. The boys continued to openly gape as Natalie and Cameron laughed and chatted and she touched his arm once or twice. Cameron had gained a nice tan in the first few weeks of summer, which made his blazing white teeth and straw-blonde hair shine even more. He wore a striped, button-down shirt, the kind that didn't even have any stains on it, and looked pretty damn presentable. He could have been on his way to a Baptism or a baby shower, but it was actually just how he lived his day-to-day life.

Cameron had beat both Ed and Bo in the Young Rising Entrepreneur competition and graduated at the top of their class. He was the kid who had his shit together, the guy who everyone knew, that dude that everyone wanted to chill with. Ed had been his friend almost as long as he had been friends with Bo, and thought he was pretty awesome. Apparently, Natalie thought that as well, judging by the way that she made deep eye contact and laughed loudly as they talked. Bo simply couldn't *stand* Cameron, and he could never exactly articulate why.

"What can I get you guys?" A familiar voice asked. Ed and Bo snapped out of their contemplation to see Hoodie Joe waiting with his notepad. They both kind of recognized him, but something was different. They stared, eyes squinting, and did not respond. Hoodie Joe sighed and lifted up the hood of his hoodie onto his head. Ed and Bo both exclaimed immediately.

"Hoodie Joe!" Bo said.

"What are you doing here, man?" Ed asked.

"For the last time, it's Hoodie Joseph," he said flatly.

"Oh. Right. Sorry," Bo mumbled. Remembering would never be their strong suit, even when they saw Hoodie Joseph every night at Square One. He was one of their first hires when they had expanded their delivery team, and it was a bit of a shock to see him during the daylight hours.

"I had to get a second job to pay for school in

the fall," Hoodie Joseph continued. Ed and Bo had never really noticed, but Hoodie Joseph looked very pale and overworked, especially in the fluorescent light of Al's Diner. He had deep bags under his eyes and a perpetually messy head of hair, although that might have been due to the hoodie. Ed and Bo both thought back to the times they had yelled at Hoodie Joseph for being late to work or slow on deliveries, and both felt guilty.

"What can I get you guys?" Hoodie Joseph asked again, more than a tad irritated. Ed resolved to yell at him less and Bo resolved to really try to remember to call him Hoodie Joseph.

"Chili bacon cheese fries," Bo said. "Thanks, Hoodie Joe. SEPH!" He yelled in overcompensation.

"Make that two. And a veggie burger. Thanks, dude." Ed added. Hoodie Joseph walked away without another word.

"Dude. Hoodie Joseph is really like a real person now," Ed remarked in wonder. He had never really thought about the fact that people could have two jobs, and it seemed very strikingly adult.

"Hoodie Joe-SEPH. Hoodie Joe-SEPH," Bo repeated to himself over and over again. Natalie finally walked back over to their booth, and the boys looked up to see Cameron heading out of the restaurant. He turned back around before he left and waved to Natalie, making the kind of eye contact that made it seem like no one else in the room mattered. She waved back, and Ed and Bo both rolled their eyes. Cameron may have been great, but no one dated Natalie without Ed's permission. At least, that's what Ed thought.

"Since when are you guys . . . talking?" Ed asked the second Natalie sat down.

"I don't want to talk about it," she said squarely. "This is absolutely none of your business."

"I'm just asking, Natalie."

"You *like* Cameron! Don't get all weird and crazy. Please. Forget all about it." Going to high school with Ed had been one of the worst things that had happened to Natalie's budding social life, and it was not at all better now that he had graduated.

"I would just like to know a few details—"

"Oh my god! Hayley Plotinsky!" Natalie shouted, and Ed instantly blushed and buried his face in his hands to hide it.

"Shit. Did she see me?" Ed asked in a panic. Bo scanned the room, searching for Hayley.

"I don't see her—Ow! I mean, there she is." Bo changed his mind when a well-aimed kick from Natalie hit him under the table. Ed continued to hide, deciding he wasn't fit to face Hayley in a shirt as stained as his was. For the next few minutes, Natalie and Bo had a lot of fun keeping Ed under the table with their running fake commentary on how close Hayley was to their table. When the chili bacon cheese fries came soon after, all the potential lovers faded into the back of each of their minds. Once again, fries were the only thing that mattered in life, and it was awesome. They were slathered in creamy cheddar cheese that made a bit of a soup at the bottom of the plate, and Ed made sure to get every last drop of cheese into his mouth. The chili was warm and melted, easily disintegrating into its bean and turkey components. The warmth of the chili seemed to burn in his stomach and literally burnt his mouth as he refused to pause to let it cool. The bacon was the star of the meal, adding the right crunch and just enough grease to ensure that Ed could not stop until he put the entire plate into his mouth.

Bo took a different approach entirely, blowing on each bite to cool it and letting the cheese and chili rest on his tongue. He closed his eyes as he went, diving into the flavors and imagining the food flowing down his throat through his stomach. The fries were canoes that carried their chili and bacon cargo down the river of cheese. It was like Niagara Falls but much more delicious. Natalie observed Ed eating faster than seemed humanly possible and Bo eating slower than a tired tortoise, and sighed as she bit into her subpar veggie burger.

"You guys, the food isn't *that* good," she murmured, but her protestations fell on deaf ears. "This is going to be a long summer."

A few real-person minutes passed, which felt like a few hours in high-person time. Ed and Bo silently delved into the world of taste buds and reveled in their sensations. After Natalie had picked at her burger as much as she wanted to, Hoodie Joseph brought over the check and broke the boys out of their fries-induced daze.

"Thanks, Hoodie . . . Joe . . . seph . . . " Bo said strenuously.

"Hoodie Joseph!" Natalie exclaimed when she saw him. "You make sure you're saving enough for some spending money too, alright?"

"Of course, Natalie," Hoodie Joseph said with a smile. Ed and Bo watched the interaction with more than a little bit of confusion. When Hoodie Joseph walked away, Ed and Bo turned to Natalie.

"What, are you dating him, too?" Ed accused.

"Oh my god. Shut up," Natalie responded. "By

the way, even if I did like Cameron, and even if I was dating him, it would be *neither* of your guys' business!" Natalie started to yell just as she stood up. "Why can't you just go to college and leave like the rest of the older brothers!"

With that, she stormed out, leaving a flabbergasted Ed and Bo staring after her. They sat in silence, unsure of what to do or say. Ed's attention slowly shifted to the remnants of the veggie burger that Natalie left in her wake, and he casually reached out to finish it.

"Women, huh?" Ed said with his mouth full of fake burger. "Can't wait to get out of here." Bo stared back at him without a smile, because they both knew that statement wasn't exactly true.

"Dude, she's our coworker now, maybe it is time that you guys stopped—" Bo began.

"She's not our coworker, she's our intern. There's a very big difference," Ed reminded him, finishing the veggie burger with a savage bite. "Since when are you on her side, anyways?"

"I'm not!" Bo quickly insisted. "Just like, we have to keep Square One running smoothly, you know?"

Ed would have kept prying, but the mention of Square One reminded him of something very important.

"Shit, dude, it's seven forty-nine. We gotta get home!" The boys threw down some money, even leaving a slightly above minimum tip for Hoodie Joseph, and ran back home for the start of their night.

"I don't know where Hayley was, man, maybe she's on vacation or something," Bo said as they sped-walked toward the garage.

"Aren't you guys friends or something?"

"She calls me 'Bo-ring' because she doesn't know my real name," Bo said flatly.

"Yeah, but it's like in a joking way. Look, I know I usually get 'mad' or whatever when you talk to her—"

"You usually kick me and tell me you'll never speak to me ever again if I say anything to her," Bo corrected.

"I don't remember that. But anyways, maybe it's time to change tactics. Maybe you get to know her, and put in a good word for me, and soon enough she orders some wine and cheese from Square One and one thing leads to another . . . " Ed trailed off, his mind in other places once more.

"Dude. How many times do I have to tell you, it's illegal for us to deliver wine when we're under twenty-one."

Ed shrugged as they walked up his driveway toward the garage. Their discussion of wooing women was tragically cut short when they reached the five people gearing up inside the garage. Natalie sat behind the desk with her head buried in stacks of papers, and barely looked up when the boys entered. In the corner, a tiny girl with short dark hair and an aura of sass surrounding her stepped forward.

"You're late," she announced, rolling her eyes.

"Terry, tone it down tonight, please," Ed retorted. "You might be the fastest biker on this side of Main Street, but you got a hell of a lot to learn about high school."

"I'm in sixth grade."

"Exactly."

Terry shrugged and leaned back, exuding a too-cool-for-school vibe even though it was the summer. The rest of the workers were from Montgomery High and in effect, Terry's elders, although they followed Terry's lead on just about everything. She was the sort of person who inspired respect through fear, and it was entirely probable she would be president one day. Hoodie Joseph stretched in the back, emitting a faint smell of fried food and processed things.

"How did you beat us here?" Bo asked incredulously. Hoodie Joseph just shrugged and gestured to his roller skates, which were his secret to speedy deliveries. Alexandra, the shy one, raised her hand in the opposite corner. She started to speak but nobody could hear her.

"What was that?" Ed asked. Alexandra repeated herself.

"One more time?" Bo said kindly.

"Are these pants okay?" she yelled, gesturing to her pinstriped black pants. "They're the only black pants I have."

"Yeah, those are chill," Bo responded. "Any other questions?"

"When do we get our uniforms?" Terry asked as she leaned against the garage door.

"I'm glad you asked," Ed answered. Ed walked over to a brown box and pulled out some cool-as-hell biker jerseys. They were red and black and adorned with the Square One logo, which was written in the speech bubble of a dragon breathing fire. A fire bubble, more accurately. Each shirt had the delivery person's last name on it. Ed displayed them proudly and then threw a jersey to each biker.

"Callums. Peterson. Ulrich. Gonzales. Henderson." He threw Terry her jersey last. She examined it intently.

"Why is there a dragon?" She finally asked.

"Because dragons are cool as hell," Bo responded. The group of bikers nodded in agreement, proudly donning their jerseys over their shirts. Ed made his way to the phone in the center of the room and ceremoniously took the cord in his hand.

"Everyone ready to open?" Ed shouted. The group murmured vague words back and Bo shook his head in visible disappointment.

"We said, 'Everyone ready to open?!'" Bo asked in an aggressive yell. The group came to life and answered a little louder. Ed and Bo both smiled at each other, and Ed plugged the phone in.

"Let's make some money," Ed declared. Everyone stared at the phone, muscles tensing. Then, the phone rang. Bo smiled broadly and picked up.

"Hello, thank you for calling Square One, what do you want?"

3

"**L**et's go, Hoodie Joe, we need an upside down cake STAT!" Ed shouted. Hoodie Joseph looked up from the double-chocolate fudge brownies he was packaging for Alexandra, who was out of breath and stretching against the garage wall.

"Shit, he means Hoodie Joseph," Bo corrected quickly Ed before Hoodie Joseph could open his mouth to retort. Alexandra continued to heave breaths in and out. "It's alright, Alexandra, catch your breath," Bo assured her. She swept her hair out of her face and nodded stoically. It was a Friday night and the people of Portland were stoned. They wanted brownies, and they wanted them now. They wanted cake, and they wanted it ten minutes ago.

"Hoodie *Joseph*! A cake that is not upright, please!" Ed shouted once more. He smiled at Bo, reveling in the newfound power. Bo weakly smiled back, mostly just worried about Alexandra's health. She looked a little bleak and burped once or twice weakly. Hoodie Joseph rolled his eyes at Ed's attempt to be a hard-ass and ran back into the kitchen. Neither Ed nor Bo could keep track of Hoodie Joseph's life outside of Square One, but they did know that he could create some kickass culinary experiments. Hoodie Joseph baked better than any boy in a hoodie they had ever met and he always seemed happiest when he was in the kitchen. Though to be fair, they were usually messing up his name outside of the kitchen, so that may have affected how happy he seemed.

Hoodie Joseph entered the kitchen with his head held high, ready to make an upside down cake as if the fate of the world hinged on it, because tonight, it did. Bo gave Alexandra a pat on the back as she climbed on her bike. She finished huffing and saluted Bo, wiping the sweat off her brow in the process. He solemnly nodded in response, and Alexandra mounted her bike and took off, laden with the precious brownie cargo. Just as Alexandra left, Terry zoomed back in.

"Hi, Square One, whatcha want?" Ed said into the phone. In peak hours, it was rare to form full sentences. When he heard the voice, he turned away from the rest of the garage and spoke in a hushed frenzy. "I can't talk right now, Mom! I'm at work!" His eyes widened. "Oh. Okay. Yeah, we could do that. Uh—it'll be right there." Ed hung up and looked at Bo with a shrug. "My Mom would like us to bring her some fresh-squeezed orange juice and a phonebook."

"For what?" Bo asked.

"I don't know, she's always doing those weird craft projects. Can you take it, please?"

"Uh, I guess so—" Before he could finish his

sentence, Ed handed Bo a fresh-squeezed glass of orange juice and Natalie threw him a phonebook. Ed was already fielding another call and shooing Bo upstairs, and so Bo had no choice but to leave. He walked slowly through the kitchen, past a frazzled Hoodie Joseph, sneezed a few times when Albert ran by, and climbed the stairs to Ms. DeLancey's study. He tentatively knocked on the door.

"Who is it?" Her voice sang back.

"Uh. Square One, Ms. DeLancey," Bo responded.

She opened the door with a goofy smile. "I know it's you, Bo," she said. "This is a cute little business you two have going!"

"Thanks, Ms. DeLancey," Bo said with a smile. He looked past her into the study, and caught sight of maps lining the wall, each with various markings and pins strewn about. In the center of the room was a board filled with different names, numbers, and pictures, and each linked to each other in some sort of web. Ms. DeLancey caught

Bo staring and smiled nervously, closing the door a bit and presenting him with money.

"Just a little crafting project!" she said. "Thanks again, Bo. Don't stay up too late!" And with that, she closed the door, leaving Bo wondering what exactly he had just seen. He had no time to reflect, however, because by the time he reentered the garage, there was a delivery of an entirely different nature to be made.

"Where have you been?" Ed yelled in a panic. "We've got a PMP. You're up, Bo." Bo nodded solemnly and took the address from Ed. He grabbed his emergency skateboard, which was only to be used in emergencies because he was clearly not skilled enough to use it at other times. Bo clumsily mounted his skateboard and sped down the driveway, glad to get out of the chaos for just a bit. Bo, the resident people-person, had started to specialize in the more specific Square One requests. He was inclined to take on all the Personal, Mental, and Philosophical queries, termed the "PMPs."

Bo sped into the night to help in a way that felt important, and left Ed to yell and deal with Terry.

"Thank you, Hoodie Joseph," Ed said when Hoodie Joseph brought out a fresh-out-of-the-oven upside-down cake. Hoodie Joseph nodded and smiled slightly with the pleasure of recognition for hard work. But then Ed continued, "For making that cake as fast as my ailing grandmother! Let's pick it up, people! We got customers waiting!" The workers in the garage rushed through their tasks, doing their best to avoid Ed's disapproval. Ed loaded up Mitchell with the upside-down cake, urging him to drive safely. They'd had too many cake-dropping incidents in the past few days to take any chances. Mitchell nodded and biked away before Ed could get any angrier, leaving just the faint trail of freshly baked sponge cake to suggest that he was ever there at all.

With the addition of Hoodie Joseph to the

Square One staff, they now officially offered fresh pastries and cakes, which was many steps ahead of Ed and Bo's clumsy attempts at baking. They had the insight to know that peanut butter covered Jello would be amazing, but now they had the baker to make it happen. Customers called in with all sorts of weird requests and obscure ideas, but Square One was all about getting people what they wanted. It did not matter how objectively bizarre an ice cream sandwich with cream cheese instead of ice cream sounded. Ed and Bo had been high enough to know to never question a weird food choice. They provided service without judgment and they made sure their staff did the same.

"Uh huh. Yep. We can make that happen. We'll get it to you as soon as we can," Ed said with finality. He hung up the phone and yelled for his master chef. "Hoodie Joseph! Can you make tacos except they're dessert and have things like candy instead of meat and chocolate instead of cheese?"

Meanwhile, Bo haphazardly skated through the dark streets, attempting a trick here and there and wiping out miserably. He didn't mind, because in his head he looked really cool. He rounded a corner and tried to nose slide on the curb, but ended up tripping forwards and landing on his nose. Luckily, his body was very used to such abuse, and he just jumped up and shook it off. At least he still was able to land a nose slide, in a sense.

A few attempts at looking cool later, Bo was on the doorstep of his soon to be customer. He knocked on the ornate wooden door of 143 Grosvenor Street; so ornate it looked like it had been cut directly from a tree. The gigantic house was entirely dark, and Bo thought that he had probably messed up the address again. He continued knocking, knuckles growing raw with the repeated banging, hoping against hope that someone would open the door so he wouldn't have to call Ed for the address in embarrassment. After a few minutes, Bo hung his head in shame and started to walk back to his board. When he was halfway down the driveway, he heard the rusty creak of the door hinge behind him. Bo turned around to see the ornate wooden door slowly drifting open.

"Hello?" he asked tentatively, wondering if this was rumored Grosvenor Street haunted mansion. He looked up and down the block and saw no other mansions. Odds were that this building was the haunted mansion.

"Come in, quickly," a scratchy voice rasped from the depths within. Bo looked around once more and shrugged, because he was never one to not go into a haunted house. He squeezed through the ornate wooden door to find an eerie, ghostly hall within. The room was cavernous and entirely empty, save for a marble, winding staircase and a lone coat rack. No pictures or decorations were in sight—it was just a decently clean and incredibly grand foyer that looked as if no one had touched it in years. Standing in the center of the room was an old man in an eye patch. He was hunched over a bit, giving off the impression that he had a medium-intensity stomachache. He looked to be in his early eighties, but despite the obvious age, he had a full head of jet-black hair.

He limped slightly toward Bo, staring and smiling weakly.

"Hello, my boy. Follow me." He turned around and hunch-backed through the grand open room to another doorway. Bo was still a bit in awe of the reflections in the foyer and had been earnestly searching for a ghost in one of them. When he realized that the Hunchback of Grosvenor Street had left the room, Bo snapped out of his private investigation and followed the eye-patched old guy. It may have been weird and it definitely was a little spooky, but Bo had made a solemn promise to give customers what they wanted. Spooky Eye-Patched Old Guy Hunchback was no exception.

Back at the home base, Natalie and Terry were in the middle of a screaming match.

"For the last time, Terry you cannot take the pool cleaner to the Newbens!" Natalie shouted, face flushed with anger.

"You and I both know I'm the fastest biker around. I'll get that pool cleaner there faster than Mitchell. Faster than Alexandra. Definitely faster than Andres," Terry responded coolly.

"It's Tall Andres," Tall Andres corrected from the back. But no one was really listening to him.

"That'll mess up the rotation, Terry!" Natalie retorted, turning to Tall Andres. "Tall Andres. Pool cleaner. Shelf A13. Go ahead." Tall Andres nodded and grabbed the pool cleaner from the shelf, hurrying past Terry to avoid her wrath as best as he could. Just as Tall Andres headed out into the night, Ed reemerged into the garage, shouting behind him as he walked.

"Next time, Hoodie Joseph, let's try a little less clumsiness and hand-burning and a little more *cooking*, alright?" He shut the door with a slam, turning to see a reddened Natalie by the whiteboard and a sulking Terry in the corner.

"I'm quitting," Terry announced to Ed. He closed his eyes in fatigue and turned to Natalie.

"I leave you alone for two minutes—"

"She started it!"

"What kind of operations manager can't even manage operations!"

"You've never let me forget that I'm an operations manager *intern*."

"Exactly! Maybe if you didn't act like this you wouldn't be an intern!"

They continued to yell back and forth as Terry smirked in the corner. In true DeLancey fashion, Natalie had also left her business credit until the last minute. Thankfully, she was smart enough not to take part in the Young Rising Entrepreneur Competition, but she did have to be Square One's unpaid intern for the entire summer.

Back with the Spooky Eye-Patch Hunchback

of Grosvenor Street, Bo himself was hunched over a map in the study. In complete contrast to the grand open foyer, the study was dark and dingy. It smelled like a few cats had lived or maybe died in there recently. The room was lined with bookshelves from one end to the other, and each was filled with stacks upon stacks of maps. Hundreds of thousands of maps from all different years, eras, and places were stacked on top of each other, piled up to the ceiling. The back wall was filled with a huge web created from newspapers and pictures that looked not at all that different from Ed's Mom's craft project.

"I just know it's somewhere off the coast of Cusco," Spooky Eye-Patch Hunchback concluded. "By the way, you can call me Trevor."

Bo nodded, uncharacteristically silent as he considered the past few minutes they had shared. Finally, he spoke.

"So, just so we're on the same page. You think that the government has sponsored a large-scale conspiracy to distract Portlandians from a shipment full of treasure that was found in the Shanghai Tunnels under downtown Portland and it's been a secret ever since? And that they've also been enacting forced disappearances of anybody who has been involved to cover up the scandal? And also the treasure is worth billions of dollars and could change the future of Portland forever?" Bo finished, out of breath.

"That's about the size of it," Eye-Patch Trevor responded. Bo was never one to discount a conspiracy theory, even one as far-fetched as this one. Sure, Hunchback Trevor had described a story so preposterous and so ridiculous that it would even surprise Bo if it ended up being true. But Trevor had spoken with such fervor and with a glint in his eye that communicated this was important. This was his world, and Bo was a part of the key to unlocking the puzzle.

"And I need your help with this," Eye-Patch

Trevor said, pointing to the contraption in the center of the desk: a laptop computer.

"Well, first you lift up this screen," Bo explained, opening the laptop. "And then you press the little button that looks like a circle with a dumb line through it. That means power."

"Why would that mean power? What does the sun button do?" Trevor exclaimed.

"Computer designers are stupid. And that sun button just makes the screen brighter."

"Then what are lamps for anymore?" Trevor bemoaned.

"Light, I guess," Bo offered, realizing that this PMP might take a bit longer than a simple post break-up counsel.

An hour or so later, Bo shared an emotional good-bye with Spooky Eye-Patch Hunchback Trevor, promising to come visit him soon. He had taught him how to use Google Maps and Satellite view and even signed him up for Facebook. Trevor was immensely thankful and paid three times the normal PMP rate, also promising Bo a cut of the treasure when he found it. Bo headed back home on the emergency skateboard, musing about lost treasure and pirates. He arrived back at the garage to find everyone working in complete silence.

"Uh, hello?" he asked, concerned. Ed turned and just shook his head, holding a finger up to his lips. Natalie sat in the corner, typing numbers into a calculator and writing furiously. She didn't even look up at Bo's entrance. The rest of the workers stood quietly on the side of the garage, killing time on their phones. Mitchell looked up when Bo walked in and shrugged at Bo's questioning look.

"They decided to play the quiet game," Mitchell whispered. Ed spun around and laughed. "Aha! You! You're out first!"

"Well now you're out too," Bo pointed out. Ed shrugged and whistled when Bo emptied his pockets into the Square One safe—a big brown bear with a removable tummy.

"PMP went well?"

"Very well. Interestingly enough, the Eye-Patch Hunchback of Grosvenor Street let me have this when I said I knew a DeLancey." He pulled a tiny scroll out of his pocket and passed it over to Ed. Ed unraveled the paper cautiously and found a very aged map of the Portland area with the signature "DeLancey" at the bottom. Ed marveled at it for a few moments, and Natalie soon came to peer over Ed's shoulder.

"Huh. Maybe it belonged to Dad . . . ?" Ed said questioningly. He turned to look at Natalie, who stared back with thoughtful eyes. It was a semi-magical moment all around that was rudely interrupted by the shrill ring of the phone. All the delivery people had stopped to observe the map-induced moment, and everyone jumped when the phone rang. After a few moments, Ed shook his head, stuffed the scroll in his pocket, and yelled in a booming voice through the garage.

"Alright! Let's get back to work people! The quiet game is over and you all lost!"

Bo rolled his eyes and jumped to answer the phone.

"Good night guys! Great work tonight! Rest up that hamstring, Alexandra! Drink some fluids, Tall Andres!" Bo yelled as the employees of Square One filed out of the garage, exhausted after a long evening of deliveries. "Thanks for not quitting, Terry!" Terry made a rude gesture as she walked by, and continued doing so up until she jumped in her Mom's minivan, which was always waiting at the bottom of the driveway at two a.m., ready to take Terry home.

"Great stuff, guys. See you tomorrow," Ed said, feeling much calmer now that business hours were over. Their team filed out of the garage, leaving the two boys and Natalie alone with a stack of money.

"My god, this job is terrible," Natalie moaned as she plopped down on the couch. "I've never been more exhausted in my life."

"It can't be more terrible than Olive Garden, though," Bo pointed out. Natalie considered for a few moments before shrugging.

"I guess so. But there are fewer breadsticks."

"There could have been more breadsticks if Hoodie Joseph hadn't taken so long on that dough," Ed pointed out. Natalie rolled her eyes dramatically for Bo's benefit, and he chuckled just a bit. Ed looked back and forth between them and continued. "Someone's gotta take control of these guys, people! It's a madhouse out there! Terry is such a little shit!"

Natalie laughed in spite of herself. "She *is* such a little shit. I can't believe it." Ed started laughing a little as well, and then Bo joined in, and before long they were all giggling about the terror of Terry. They sat on the couch together, enjoying the lack of standing, and Bo pulled out the only thing Ed wanted in the entire world: a bag of salt and vinegar chips. Ed beamed wide as he pulled out the only thing Bo was missing in his life: a pre-rolled joint. Natalie just watched the bizarre ritualistic exchange of gifts and hoisted herself up out of her seat.

"I'll see you guys tomorrow. I've got a thing so I might be kind of late for work tomorrow," she said as she moved toward the door.

"What kind of thing?" Ed asked sharply.

"Is it with Cameron?" Bo asked with more than a touch of worry.

"It's not *not* with Cameron," she said coyly. Bo struggled to wrap his head around the double negatives in that sentence as Natalie turned around and headed back inside. "Calm down, both of you," she said as she walked away. "I'm just protesting the gender binary in public restrooms down at City Hall."

That left Ed and Bo both speechless, because they did not understand many of those words in that order in that sentence. Ed eventually shrugged and began to shovel chips into his mouth while Bo blew out rings of smoke. They sat back and relaxed, laughing about the weird requests they had and the strange people they'd met and how much of a shit Terry was. One bag of salt and vinegar chips became two, then three, and before long, the boys were licking the remnants of chip dust off their fingers because they *needed* more of that delicious taste-bud excursion. One joint turned into two, then three, and before long, the boys were ready for a long run of cartoon watching before an even longer run of sleeping. The graduate life was treating them quite well, and they didn't even remember to try to remember what they had forgotten about that trip they were supposed to go on with Paolo. In fact, it was starting to feel like they had simply dreamed the whole thing.

4

"**S**o, that's why you'll have to spend another year with us," Belfroy said with an eerie grin. He sat behind his desk, hands firmly clasped and head cocked slightly to the side. Ed and Bo sat in the two chairs that they had thought they had escaped forever.

"No way," Bo said, shaking his head in protest.

"We already graduated!" Ed yelled, the fear rising in his throat. Belfroy grinned back at them, shaking his head ever so slightly.

"Well, you see, you forgot about the credit in prom." Ed and Bo looked at each other, both a bit confused.

"But prom is optional!" Bo shouted, sweat beginning to form at his brow. "And we didn't have dates!"

Belfroy continued to shake his head and made a slight "tsking" noise as he did so. "It's a well-known rule in public high school education that you must attend prom with a date of the opposite sex in order to graduate well-adjusted and happy," he paused, pointing up at the cat dangling from the wire above his head. "How else can we be sure that you'll hang in there?"

Ed dropped his head into his hands and Bo ran his hands through his hair rapidly. They looked at each other with stress blackouts, both of them profusely sweating and terribly anxious. Terror Town would be their home forever.

"Each of you *must* ask the woman you're most afraid of asking to Summer Slam," Belfroy continued. "You know who that is."

Ed and Bo both froze in panic.

"I cannot even think about asking Hayley," Ed groaned.

"There's no way I can—" Bo started, before stopping himself abruptly. "Uh, never mind."

"Who are you afraid to ask?" Ed asked curiously, but Bo saved himself in the only way he knew how.

"This is a dream!" Bo shouted loudly, and just at that moment, he rolled off the couch and onto his face on the garage floor. Bo's nose began to leak blood at a slightly alarming pace.

"Dude," Bo said, clutching his bloody nose.

"Dude," Ed answered, drenched in sweat.

"I just had the weirdest dream!" they said at the exact same time. And well, whenever that happened, they had no choice but to honor the tradition as old as time.

"Jinx!" They both yelled. The garage was an easy playing field, especially since everything had been labeled and organized in recent weeks. They both lurched for the Snacks and Drinks shelf, subset, Soda. Bo was a bit blinded by the blood that was now streaming out of his nose and tripped over his own feet. Ed jumped over the fallen body of Bo and grabbed a ginger ale.

"You owe me a soda!" Ed yelled triumphantly, not really noticing that Bo was now clutching both his nose and his ankle in excruciating pain. Ed opened the soda happily and sat back down on the couch, letting Bo figure his shit out on his own.

"It doesn't really work as well when we already own the soda," Bo mumbled through his fingers, using his t-shirt to wipe the blood off his face. Unfortunately he was wearing a white shirt, so the blood very noticeably smeared and stained his shirt, leaving him looking like the recent perpetrator of a very bloody crime. He pushed himself up off the cold garage floor and dramatically limped back to the couch, sighing heavily as he sat down. The boy just wanted some attention, but Ed couldn't be bothered to stop enjoying his ginger ale long enough to empathize. After a bit of silent soda enjoying on Ed's part, Bo turned to Ed.

"I can't believe we had the same dream," Bo said, still in a daze from the blood loss.

"Yeah . . . " Ed said hesitantly. "With Belfroy?"

"And prom!" Bo said.

"And not being able to graduate?" Ed asked a little more confidently.

"And how we have to ask girls to the prom," Bo continued.

"And accidentally kissing in the dark at Summer Slam! I'm so glad you dreamed that too. Weird, right?" Ed said with a relieved laugh.

"Wait. What?" Bo said, shaking his head a little.

"Uhhh . . . I mean . . . "

Ed and Bo looked at each other and silently realized that maybe they hadn't been dreaming the same dream after all.

"No, that's not what happened," Ed continued, flustered. Bo just smiled and pulled out the DinoBong.

"It happens, man. I've had like six of those dreams before," Bo said and Ed shrugged in agreement. Bo gestured to the DinoBong.

"Shall we?" Bo asked. Bo always asked the important questions.

"We shall," Ed answered. Bo smiled and filled the dinosaur with the last few buds in their weed baggy. A few DinoHits later, all potentially incriminating dreams about Summer Slam or kissing each other were far in the back of their minds and a much more pressing issue was facing them.

"Dude. We gotta hit up Doug the Dealer," Bo said, smile dropping just a bit. A visit to Doug was never exactly the easiest thing to do—he preferred to communicate about drugs in "alternative" ways. After all these years, they still hadn't seen Doug's face, and Bo was starting to get fed up with having to learn a new language every time he wanted some drugs. But alas, in their neighborhood, Doug the Drug Dealer cornered the market.

"It's definitely your turn," Ed said, lighting up the DinoBong and breathing in deeply, holding the smoke in his lungs for as long as he physically could before coughing it out vehemently.

"No way! I had to do sign language with that convenience store clerk two weeks ago," Bo responded.

"I feel like I just learned rudimentary Danish to decode that whole post-it note trail Doug left . . . " Ed said, trailing off. "Fine. I'll make the call."

As Bo took a lingering hit, savoring the end of the stash, Ed reluctantly dialed the number, which gave him a menu option, which led him to a BestBuy where he asked for the distributions manager, which gave him a series of dial tones, which he ticked off on a pad of paper. After a few minutes he hung up and announced, "Six p.m. tomorrow at the paper supply store on Elm Street."

Bo cackled at his misfortune. "Dude. You're probably going to have to communicate through origami or some shit."

Ed sighed and hung his head. He took a hit and sunk lower into the couch.

"Maybe I should order a tele*gram*," he said, which made both of them chuckle for quite a few minutes. When silence fell, Bo cleared his throat importantly.

"But we're getting more than a gram, right?"

"Of course, of course," Ed assured him.

Just when the age-old salt and vinegar urge began to strike, Ed and Bo were both startled by a knock on the garage door.

"Are we expecting anyone?" Bo asked.

"I don't even know what day it is, man," Ed said. Bo pulled himself up and pressed the button that began the slow ascent of the archaic garage door. The door shook and rattled and emitted a terrifying screeching noise as it slowly rose. They saw two feet, adorned in shiny black dress shoes, then legs clad in well-fitting black pants, then a sturdy black belt, then a light blue dress shirt under a dark blue suit jacket, and finally, the charming face of Paolo Müllers.

"Hello, my boys," he said. They were a bit surprised to see him, but mostly also surprised that it was dark outside.

"Is it night time or day time?" Ed asked.

"It's seven fifty-four!" He said urgently. Ed and Bo looked at each other, sensing this had something to do with that trip they were supposed to go on.

"Right," Ed said slowly.

"And of course, *we* know what that means," Bo said cautiously. "But do you understand, Paolo?"

"You're ready, right?" Paolo asked without a smile.

Ed and Bo once again exchanged a significant look.

"Oh, of course," Bo said.

"We've been ready for like . . . days, if not weeks," Ed declared.

"Great!" Paolo said, jumping toward the limo. "Then let's head to the airport!"

Ed and Bo glanced at their decrepit attire and their lack of packing. They saw Terror Town close by once more, and Ed felt his breaking point.

"Hey, Paolo?" Ed said nervously. "We, uh, we

don't exactly remember where we're supposed to go or when or what this trip is for or any of that," he said in one huge breath. Paolo burst out laughing, but then his face fell as he looked back and forth between Ed and Bo's guilty expressions.

"Uh, right. Okay. No problem," Paolo said tentatively. "You boys have a lot going on these days. Sit down, please. Let me pitch it to you." Ed and Bo felt the weight of the secret rise off of them and they collapsed on the couch in relief; the deceit had almost been too much. Paolo went to the beanbag chair and perched, procuring two bags of salt and vinegar chips from his jacket and tossing them to the boys.

"Calm down, it's okay. All you gotta do is eat and listen," he said. Ed and Bo nodded, because those were two things they were quite good at. "As you know, I represent Mr. Savage at the CotLaw Corporation. They do venture capital and investments in young companies they think are worth something." Paolo leaned in with emphasis, his white teeth sparkling as he spoke. "Now here is where it gets interesting. They want to invest in you."

Ed and Bo continued to eat chips in enraptured silence, for the first time focusing more on words than on the taste of their beloved snack. Neither of them really knew what "invest" meant, but it sure sounded like a good thing.

"Yes, right now you're very low-scale. Very local, very handmade. But that's the kind of image CotLaw is looking for. They—" he paused and smiled, "*we* want to keep the local edge but make you big. Regional. National. Eventually—international. You boys ever been to Tokyo?" Ed and Bo shook their heads, still continuously chomping through their chips. "You'll love it." The boys nodded, because of course they would love Tokyo, especially when Paolo said it the way he did.

"But don't just take my word for it. We are going to fly you guys out to the headquarters in Silicon Valley. That's right, California. The place with the sexiest beaches, sexiest parties, and," he paused for emphasis, "sexiest ladies. Any questions?" Paolo looked from Ed to Bo, who stared back. Both of them were really high and were having trouble focusing. Ed kept imagining himself in a suit like Paolo's and wondered if he would finally get tan in California. Bo was still deeply engrossed in the salt and vinegar, feeling like he could maybe see his future in the chips. Maybe it was the weed or maybe it was all the talk about the future or maybe it was just the chips—but he looked at each chip before he ate it and saw some shit. One chip had a warm sunny beach in which he was sitting on a hammock next to Ed. The next chip showed him finally mastering surfing in the Californian waves. In the third chip he saw himself walking down a palm tree-lined street, hand in hand with Natalie.

Bo looked up and realized he most certainly did have a question. He hesitantly raised his hand.

"Yes, Bo."

"Do they have salt and vinegar chips there?"

"They do. Good question." Ed raised his hand.

"Ed."

"Will we get to eat salt and vinegar chips there?"

"Yes, equally good question." Ed and Bo nodded in satisfaction. Now Ed was picturing himself in Paolo's suit eating chip after chip in a huge executive room and Bo was seeing chip after chip of him and Natalie lounging in California together.

"Any non salt and vinegar chips related questions?" The boys shook their heads.

"Great. Don't decide yet about the acquisition—" he paused and smiled at their fearful lack of comprehension. "That's a fancy term for CotLaw partnering with Square One. Anyways, you have a whole week to decide. So, in the meantime, let's get going." He stood up abruptly and gestured at the limo outside. "Our ride, boys."

"Like, right now?" Ed asked. He hadn't asked his Mom yet and had just made an appointment to go to a paper company for some drugs tomorrow. Bo looked at his bloodstained t-shirt and decided maybe he needed to change first.

"It's now or never, boys. Opportunities don't wait forever," Paolo said with a smile, heading toward the limo. "Also I told you about this weeks ago! Mr. Savage does not like to be rescheduled."

Ed and Bo both hesitated on the couch.

"But we're not packed!" Ed shouted.

"And I'm covered in blood!" Bo added.

"We'll buy you new clothes, don't you worry!" Paolo yelled back, opening the door to the limo and yelling out one last time. "Hurry up boys, the plane doesn't wait for anyone!"

Ed and Bo eyed each other anxiously.

"Dude. Can we . . . " Bo trailed off.

"I don't know, man. It's crazy." Ed answered.

"What about the business?"

"I guess . . . Natalie could take over?" Ed said tentatively.

"Oh, yeah. Would she be cool with that?" Bo asked, eternally fearful of doing anything not cool to Natalie.

"Who knows? Probably. She's gotta earn her business credit somehow," Ed declared.

The limo beeped twice.

"It would be pretty awesome to go to California . . ." Ed said, picturing himself in the suit.

"And we don't have to actually decide anything . . ." Bo added.

"I'll leave Natalie a note," Ed said, scrawling quickly on a scrap of paper. "And we'll call her from the limo and get everything squared away."

"More like Squared One away, am I right?" Bo said with a chuckle.

"Dude. You're so right," Ed nodded.

The limo beeped once more.

"Let's go to California?" Ed asked.

"Let's go to California," Bo answered. They headed out to the limo without looking back.

5

"Oh yeah, I was just kidding about the whole 'plane doesn't wait for anybody,' thing," Paolo said with a wry smile as the limo pulled up to a tiny black jet with the words "COTLAW CORPORATION" emblazoned on the side of the plane in gold. The boys stared out the window in awe. Sitting on real leather seats in the limo had almost been too much fanciness for one day, and now there was a whole plane to deal with. Ed and Bo were basically entirely won over before they even stepped foot in the plane, and luckily for them, the fun was just beginning. Paolo smiled as he saw the boys' wide-eyed reaction.

"Dude," Bo whispered to Ed.

"I know," Ed whispered back. They fist-bumped ceremoniously and stepped out of the car, Paolo hovering behind them.

"I love this part," Paolo said to himself as the door to the jet opened and two beautiful women stepped out to welcome them.

"Mr. Müllers," the brunette said, nodding with recognition.

"Ed, Bo," both women said in unison. Ed and Bo were astonished that they knew their names, and they muttered the only thing that came to mind.

"Jinx," both boys said at the same time, before looking at each other and shouting out a second jinx. Sure, they were on a private plane ordered by one of the richest companies in the world. Yeah, they were on a business trip that required that they talk and act like adults. Of course, they wanted to succeed and do well and all that jazz. But nothing stopped them from fulfilling the sacred jinx requirement.

Ed and Bo both bolted onto the plane, madly searching for soda. Paolo followed after them, confused and a bit alarmed. The women asked if they should do anything, and Paolo just shook his head. Ed and Bo burst through the cabin doors, and funnily enough, neither of them had to look very hard for a soda. The plane was lined, wall-to-wall, with snacks and drinks. Four luxurious seats stood in the center of the plane, and instead of regular airplane walls, every few inches had a pouch with a different kind of snack or treat or drink in it. Ed and Bo stood, gawking in amazement. Ed walked to the left end of the plane, Bo walked to the right end, and they each absentmindedly plucked a soda out of the wall, throwing it to the other one and resolving their jinx quite peacefully. The boys were in a flying snack-mobile and it was everything they'd ever dreamed of.

"Welcome to your ride, my boys," Paolo said, smiling at the dumbfounded boys. "Please, take a seat, and we'll be on our way." Ed and Bo walked over to their seats, equipped with the same kind of luxurious leather that the limo seats were covered in. They sat down, reveling in a seat that wasn't from a thrift store.

"Dude. This is so much better—" Ed began.

"Than the couch. I know," Bo finished. They laughed and fist-bumped again before reaching over and tearing down salt and vinegar chips from the walls. Paolo sat down across from them, folding his legs and leaning back into his seat.

"I told you guys I'd take care of you. Now. For the inflight entertainment, we have two options."

"Don't you mean on-ground entertainment?" Bo asked with a grin.

"Look out the window." Ed and Bo leaned over to the window to see that they were, in fact, already in the air.

"Oh, wow. I'm not used to planes taking off without thirty announcements," Bo said in a small voice.

"Anyways. Our inflight entertainment options:

on our left, we have Liz and Madison." He gestured to the brunette and the blonde who had welcomed them onto the plane. Liz and Madison waved hello, tipping their little stewardess hats when Ed and Bo waved back. The women were clad in pale blue skirts and tight, white tops with the word "CotLaw" emblazoned on it. They were stewardesses, but not the kind you saw on Delta. Ed gulped and adjusted his glasses and Bo just shifted his legs a little bit uncomfortably. Neither of them had actually seen a woman, a real woman, who wasn't a teacher or a mom in real life before. It was kind of incredible.

"And on our right, we have . . . " he gestured to a tiny disk on top of a small table. Ed and Bo squinted, trying to make out what it was. Ed's eyes suddenly widened as the realization dawned on him.

"The new Badge of Honor game!" He shouted, jumping up excitedly. Liz gestured for Ed to buckle his seatbelt, and he apologized and settled back down into the chair. Ed turned to Paolo excitedly.

"It doesn't even come out until March!" Ed cried.

"Luckily for us, CotLaw partners with the production company that makes the Badge of Honor games," Paolo said smugly.

Ed and Bo gazed in wonder at all of the gunfighting, soldier-saving, and duty-fulfilling action contained in that one tiny disk. They were so immersed they hardly heard when Paolo asked, "Your decision, boys?"

"The game," Ed said without hesitation.

"Absolutely," Bo agreed. Paolo looked just a little crestfallen, and shook his head slightly to Liz and Madison. Two screens descended from the ceiling in front of Ed and Bo, and Paolo gestured to their arm rests.

"Go ahead, open it." Ed cautiously touched a button on the armrest and it popped open to reveal a controller. Bo did the same, laughing when the armrest popped up.

"Dude, it's like a jack in the box," he said

through his chuckles. Ed did not respond because he was singularly focused on starting the game. Paolo clapped twice and the lights dimmed, and then he clapped four times and the game began.

"Everything is clap activated on this plane, boys. It's the way of the future," Paolo told them, but his words fell on deaf ears. Ed was already intently immersed in the game, crawling through a tunnel towards his first gun. Bo sat and watched in rapture, but did not pick up his controller.

"Don't you want to play, Bo?" Paolo asked. Bo just shook his head in response. "I like to observe," he said in a daze. He was a watcher, not a fighter. Paolo shrugged, leaned back, and clapped five times. Madison came out and placed eyeshades over his eyes, and he thanked her with that same dazzling smile.

The hour and a half plane ride seemed to pass faster than Ed and Bo thought possible. They could have stayed on the plane playing Badge of Honor for the rest of their lives, assuming an unlimited supply of salt and vinegar chips. When the plane touched down, Paolo lifted up his eyeshades and had the unpleasant task of tearing the two boys away from the most exciting thing they'd ever played.

"This. Is. Awesome," Ed said, not taking his eyes away from the screen.

"Can we stay here forever?" Bo asked. Paolo chuckled and rose to his feet, clapping in different combinations a few different times, which turned the lights back on, called out Liz and Madison, and much to the boys' dismay, sent the screens back up into the ceiling. They yelled in protest, but Paolo shushed them good-naturedly.

"Boys, boys, boys. You'll each get a copy of the game when we land back in Portland, alright?" They considered this for a few moments.

"As long as you promise," Bo demanded.

"Hey. Come on. I'm your friend. You guys can trust me!" Paolo said, holding out two bags of salt and vinegar chips. He knew the exactly right way to make peace, and so when Liz and Madison opened the cabin doors to reveal a cool Californian night, Ed and Bo didn't even mind leaving. Ed, Bo, and Paolo walked down the landing ramp, the boys imagining that they were in some sort of superhero or action adventure movie. Ed and Bo even began to adopt the confident swagger of Paolo—he was a dude who knew how to walk. They shadowed him across the landing pad, turning to wave to Liz and Madison, who waved back warmly.

"Don't worry, you'll see them again," Paolo said, without looking back. He brushed his hands through his jet-black hair and kept walking. Ed and Bo struggled to keep up as they walked in Paolo's shadow across the roof to an elevator.

"Shit!" Bo said when his mind returned to the place it usually did in moments of transition. "We need to call Natalie!"

"Oh, damn. Yeah. Okay, we'll just ask to borrow a phone—" but Ed was cut off by the man who was very used to interrupting people.

"So, here's how this week will look, boys. Keep

up and follow me and you'll be fine," Paolo inter-jected, not stopping to look back. "We're going on an adventure, if you will. CotLaw likes to show its potential clients what they're all about, so for you two, that means a lot of looking and enjoying."

"We're good at that," Bo huffed, running out of breath a little. They reached the elevator and Paolo pushed the ground level.

"I know, that's only part of the reason they've chosen you. I'll be in meetings on your behalf for most of the week, but we'll meet back up at the end to discuss the nuts and bolts of that tedious con-tract. In the meantime, a good friend of mine and the best writer in the business will be looking after you." The elevator neared the ground level and Bo saw his chance.

"Do you think that we could maybe borrow a pho—" but he was halted in his tracks when the elevator door dinged open and a young woman in a gray pinstriped suit stared back at them with eyes that seemed to be filled with fire.

"Whatever he's been saying about me, don't believe it," the woman said with a wry smile. Paolo smiled back and stepped off the elevator to hug her. Ed and Bo also stepped off the elevator, but could only stand and wait awkwardly, gaping at this compelling woman who looked way too familiar. She had jet-black hair that was tied up tight in a bun, sensible glasses, and an angular face. Her confident lean and effortless way of existing exuded such an intoxicating aura that Ed and Bo couldn't look away. Part of the intoxicating aura might have been the rose-petal infused waft of air that seemed to surround her in a bubble, but the rest was just the overwhelming power of this mysterious woman. She looked Ed and Bo up and down, which made them both tinge with excitement.

"I don't bite," she said with a smile. They chuckled, immediately put at ease by her disarming mouth and the softness hidden behind the fire in her eyes.

"My cousin, Rosalie. Rosalie, my newest business associates, Ed and Bo." Ed and Bo shook

Rosalie's hand in turn. Bo suddenly became very aware of the fact that his t-shirt was still blood-stained, but unfortunately, he had very little power to do anything about it. Ed wondered if he had put on deodorant this morning. He hadn't.

"Rosalie will take care of you this week. She'll show you the lifestyle. She'll show you what CotLaw has to offer," Paolo drawled, eyeing the boys closely.

"Welcome to California, boys," Rosalie added. Paolo grinned, clapped both boys on their backs, and then ran off in a different direction, shouting as he went.

"Don't get them into too much trouble, Rose!"

"No promises!" She yelled back. When Paolo had disappeared around the corner, Rosalie sighed a long sigh of relief.

"Now that he's gone, the real fun can begin," she said as she leaned in closer to both of the boys. They instinctively flinched back, because they had never been that close to a real woman before. Her fire eyes glinted, as she looked them up and down once more. Ed and Bo had never felt more naked, not even when they had to do that naked lap that one time they had gone to a party and lost really badly at beer pong.

"Calm down you two, you look like ghosts," she said in a velvety voice that did nothing to calm down either of them.

"I can't tell if this is heaven or hell," Ed whispered to Bo.

"Both."

Rosalie shook her head amicably and beckoned to the boys. "We have a long week ahead of us with a lot to talk about. I, for one, cannot wait." She meandered off at a calming place, slow enough for Ed and Bo to finally keep up. Thoughts of Square One and Natalie faded to the dark recesses of their adolescent minds, because right now, only one woman mattered. Ed and Bo locked eyes as they followed what may be the most interesting woman they'd ever met and did the only thing they could at a time like this. They shrugged and kept walking.

6

"**S**o you're a writer, then?" Ed asked Rosalie at dinner. They were sitting in a beautiful open-air café that was filled with young attractive Californians who loved to eat dinner at a late hour. Ed and Bo hadn't eaten since the sixteen bags of chips on the plane, so they were quite hungry and glad to be eating something that wasn't from Al's Diner or Ms. DeLancey's canned food collection.

"A reporter, technically," she answered. She was brisk and to the point, and somehow still effortlessly comfortable. "But I freelance for CotLaw, too." Ed nodded, enraptured by Rosalie's no-nonsense style of talking. He was far from the ties of high school and Al's Diner, and thoughts of Hayley Plotinsky began to fade from his mind. He couldn't even really remember what color her hair was or what her eyes were like because right now, all he could picture was Rosalie. Probably mostly because she was sitting right in front of him, but maybe Ed didn't have the energy for undying unrequited love anymore. He wasn't a kid; he was a high school graduate and he knew enough about women to know that you had to be in the same state as them to even have a shot at having sex.

Ed gazed off into space, picturing the aforementioned sex and pinching himself every so often so he didn't get too obviously riled. He looked as if he had a nervous twitch, but maybe that was just what being a virgin was. Bo noticed his best friend's dreamy gaze towards the left and had more than an inkling of what he was thinking. He knew Ed and he knew Ed's gross daydreams even better, because he had to sit through detailed descriptions of them ever since they discovered you could delete your Internet history after watching porn.

He knew what Ed was thinking because he knew Ed, but also partially because he himself was thinking similar thoughts. He wasn't a kid either, and maybe in the time apart his love for Natalie had faded in comparison to what he felt for the effortlessly beautiful and overwhelmingly composed Rosalie. He started to gaze to the left as well, mind delving into the depths of his expansive imagination with someone other than Natalie for the first time in quite a while. The three sat in silence, Ed and Bo simultaneously thinking thoughts that would make everyone else blush. Rosalie stared back at the oddly dressed and moderately smelly boys, examining them and scribbling a few notes down in her notepad. The boys would have recognized her notepad as the same one Paolo had back in their business development meetings if they had been paying attention. But when you put teenage boys directly across from a beautiful woman with eyes of fire, they will often miss some details.

"Boys? What do you think?" Rosalie asked once more, snapping Ed and Bo out of their revelry.

"Uh . . . " Bo trailed off, looking to Ed in panic.

"We think . . . " Ed began and then trailed off into nothingness.

"I think you can do it. In fact, it'd be stupid not to," Rosalie added. Ed and Bo nodded a little bit less confidently. They weren't sure if they were agreeing to sign their lives away but it didn't matter, because no matter what, they would always agree with Rosalie.

"Great," she said when their nodding had gone on for sufficiently long. The boys' voices caught in their throats. Ed silently prayed that he didn't sell the company and his family's house. Bo remembered that they hadn't called Natalie yet and swore he would call her if they got out of this alive. Rosalie gestured to the waiter, who came over with his pad in hand.

"One of everything!" She said with a smile. The waiter nodded with wide eyes and scurried away into the kitchen. Ed and Bo both breathed expansive sighs of relief.

"One of everything," Bo agreed with a smile.

"We can *totally* do that," Ed murmured. The boys were both thoroughly relieved they had not accidentally agreed to sign away their company.

"I heard you boys like food," Rosalie said simply.

A few dozen minutes and a few dozen plates of food later, Ed and Bo sat back in harmony, content to the fullest. Their mouths tinged with the faint heat of the Asian fusion they had just scarfed down—one of everything was quite a tall order when the menu had sixty-three items.

"That was amazing," Bo said with a slight burp. Rosalie smiled and agreed wholeheartedly, although in the boys' feeding frenzy she had barely gotten to eat any of the food.

Rosalie leaned in, causing that same kind of flutter in both of the boys even though they also felt the flutter of a shitload of food. "CotLaw owns this restaurant," she said. "I come here four times a week," she admitted with a laugh. Thoughts of eating here four times a week with Rosalie flashed through both boys' minds—though in Ed's mind, Bo wasn't there, and in Bo's mind, Ed wasn't there either.

"Are you tired?" Rosalie asked as she flipped through the notebook.

"A little," Bo admitted.

"Not at all," Ed countered. Bo felt his face flush just a little, and suddenly, he wasn't tired either.

"Me neither, actually. I'm great," Bo corrected himself.

"Yeah, I'm awesome. I could stay up all night," Ed continued.

"Not if I stay up all night first!" Bo said. They both smiled back at Rosalie as if she was the only one that mattered, because well, she was.

"I know the perfect place," Rosalie said with finality as she reached the page in the notebook

she was looking for. She dropped down the company card, charged the meal, and ushered the boys back into the company limo, which always seemed to be lurking nearby. Ed and Bo piled into the car, although this time, they didn't naturally make eye contact and grin about the new exciting thing that was happening. Some new feeling was growing, and they were both equally confused at its unfamiliarity. It definitely wasn't a pretty feeling and it seemed to come from a dark place inside of them, one that they didn't even really know they had until this moment. It made each of them want to be the one who could stay awake the latest. It made Ed want to mock Bo for his poor skateboarding skills and it made Bo want to make sure that everyone knew Ed watched an inordinate amount of Internet porn. It made Bo talk a little bit louder and it made Ed walk a little bit faster.

They each needed Rosalie to laugh at their joke and smile at them with her fire eyes more than th other. As they rode in the car to their unidentifi

destination, they told stories over each other and sat up a bit straighter and got a bit angrier than normal. They didn't exactly know they had a shared crush, but on some level, they sensed it. For the very first time, they were on opposite sides, but not in the straightforward video game kind of way.

"Welcome, boys, to CotLaw's premiere SkateCade," Rosalie announced as the car pulled up to what looked like an empty amusement park. The boys gaped in response, which they had been doing a fair amount of recently.

"Yes, that's right. Before us lies a combination skate park and arcade," she said warmly. After a few moments of tingly silence, she reached over the boys, which made them tingly in a whole different kind of way, and opened the door.

"Well? What are you waiting for?"

Ed and Bo needed no further encouragement. They stumbled out of the car into the warm Californian air and entered their nirvana. A combination skate park and arcade turned out to be

exactly as it sounds: completely amazing. Half-pipes, ramps, rails, and empty pools surrounded various video-game booths and machines. For the skateboarder, there was everything one could want: awesome music, huge stadium lights to keep the nighttime out, and a hell of a lot of ground to skate on. It was also pristine and filled with brand new rails to be shred and stairs to be conquered. For the video game enthusiast, look no further. From the classic arcade style video games to the newest multi-player Badges of Honor game, the arcade was very much fully stocked. It was spread throughout the SkateCade, with the game-playing stations proceeding in increasing order from their release date. It was incredibly well designed, ingenious, and completely empty.

"CotLaw owns this too," Rosalie said behind them. Ed and Bo both jumped, kind of forgetting that she was there. Not even Rosalie could distract them from the beauty that lay in front of them.

"Dude," breathed Bo in awe.

"Dude," answered Ed.

Bo went for the skateboarding first and Ed went straight to Badge of Honor. As Ed settled in, pulling down his voice-command headset and picking up his controller in one of the comfiest gaming couches he'd had the pleasure of sitting on, Bo was in the process of tearing up the half-pipe. They were like kids in a candy shop—well, later, they literally were, because that's what the SkateCade's snack bar had to offer: candy. As Bo started to conquer the empty pool and Ed unlocked a new level, they were both the happiest they had ever been. Sure, the opening night of Square One had been pretty badass. Ed's eighteenth birthday—that was fun, too. But the SkateCade, that was a whole new world of happiness. Rosalie sat in a comfy couch in the snack bar area, watching the various security cameras littered throughout the park and searching through her green notepad. Her face remained impassively blank, though at a few of

Bo's "hell, yeah!" exclamations and Ed's uproarious celebrations she grinned ever so slightly.

Several hours later, Bo had tired himself out enough and hurt his pride with some pretty epic falls a few dozen too many times. He switched to the Arcade games, starting at the old school end, because in his words, those kinds of games were "easier to understand." Ed had started to get carpel tunnel syndrome from his hours of intense gaming, and so had decided to give the whole "skateboarding" thing another go. After a few nervous attempts to move forwards, he remembered why he didn't like to skateboard in the first place, and luckily, the SkateCade was prepared for that exact situation. Right next to the row of skateboards stood a majestic line of scooters. Ed smiled, picked out the green one, and started to kind of enjoy outdoor activity for once. When Bo saw Ed dare to drop down into the empty pool on the scooter, he darted out and grabbed his skateboard, following suit. For the next couple of hours, they played a whole variety of skating games, most of them just made up as they went along. None of the games ended without some sort of physical pain, but at least in these games, everyone was a winner. Or maybe, everyone was a loser, but at least everyone was equal. Back in the SkateCade snack bar, Rosalie munched on some Skittles and smiled a little bit bigger as the shouts of joy and sights of merriment filled the air.

Finally, it was nearing the real nighttime hours and the boys were too exhausted to even pretend that they were not. They returned their boards, controllers, and scooters and promptly collapsed on the big couches in the snack bar.

Ed and Bo felt like they had lived an entire week, but in real person time, it had only been four hours. "That's just how time works here at CotLaw," Rosalie explained when the boys voiced their complete time displacement. "Everyone is always kind of working, yet always also mostly not working." Ed and Bo put this piece of advice into their back pocket for later to use at Square

One. Rosalie took them back to their hotel after the SkateCade and sent them up to their room to get changed for the evening.

"Don't take too long," she said as they headed toward the elevator. "We've got a full night—a visit to CotLaw and a meeting with Mr. Savage himself." The boys nodded, too fatigued to respond.

"Sorry for the late hour," Rosalie said, "But that's how CotLaw does things. We tend to work late. I know it must be a little weird—"

"No, actually, that's pretty much exactly how we do things," Ed said with a laugh.

"Well, then. We must be a perfect fit," Rosalie responded, and when she looked Ed in the eyes he felt like they could be a perfect fit another way as well.

"Yep. All three of us. What a perfect fit," Bo jealously interjected. Ed shot him a look and Bo shot him a look back and then it was time to head to the hotel room. The boys trudged upstairs, excited to clean themselves, for once.

"Let's call Natalie when we get up there," Ed said as way of peace offering.

"Oh shit! Yeah. We totally have to tell her that we left," Bo agreed.

But all thoughts of Natalie were again vanquished when the boys reached Room 7G. It was a serene oasis of luxury of which Ed and Bo could have never even dreamed, let alone imagine.

"This room is not messing around," Bo murmured as he stared in the doorway.

"You can say that again," Ed responded, also gazing in awe.

"This room is not messing around," Bo repeated, smiling at Ed like he used to before Rosalie. Ed smiled back. In front of them was a white, cushioned, high-class heaven. Every single item of furniture was white with a subtle gold trim, and it made for quite an impressive layout. The entryway boasted white and gold tile floor, complete with white and gold ornamental wolves guarding the door. The living room followed, which was carpeted with the kind of fluffy carpeting that belonged in front of a fireplace in the winter. Also, there was an entire wall of the living room that was made out of a television. White and gold couches and beanbag chairs gracefully shaped the room and on opposite sides were the doors to two identical master suites.

Ed and Bo sprinted from room to room, exclaiming at the purity and the fanciness of it all. They marveled at the TV and each claimed a bedroom— and then promptly ran to the other bedroom to make sure that everything was the same. They turned on the Jacuzzi bathtubs and made sure to touch everything they saw. They felt the smooth and hard marble counter tops, they felt the airy and fluffy white rugs, they felt the bed made out of clouds, and most importantly, they felt the handle to the mini fridge.

This wasn't just any mini fridge. This was a mini fridge that was not for making things cold, but rather was for the preservation of salt and vinegar chips. Ed and Bo collapsed onto the center white and gold leather couch, giggling with giddiness. They looked at each other, and their eyes said it all. Only one thing could possibly make this any better. Ed reached into his backpack for the only supplies they had packed and pulled out the DinoBong, some rolling papers, and a lighter. But his face fell that deep shade of white when he continued to tear through his backpack, the kind of white that meant the world might end soon.

"What is it?" Bo asked, panic starting to strike him too.

"We never picked up from Doug the Dealer," Ed said, voice flat with the empty realization that they were in the best place on earth with no weed. Bo was struck silent as he went through a rollercoaster of emotions: fear, anxiety, and terror, before finally settling on hunger. He knew where to find the only thing that could provide even a hint of solace. Bo headed to the mini fridge and pulled out two bags of salt and vinegar chips, passing one to Ed. Ed nodded solemnly, a tear welling in his eye.

But when the boys opened up the bags, they found something even better than chips. They always said nothing would ever be better than salt and vinegar chips, but they had never looked into a bag of chips and seen a bag full of weed.

Ed smiled at Bo and Bo smiled back. Fifteen minutes later, Ed and Bo were giggling again, but only partially from giddiness. They moved to their new favorite positions—Ed on his back directly next to the television wall, and Bo sitting cross-legged, staring at the wolf.

"Holy shit, Ed!" Bo yelled from the entryway.

"What, man?" Ed yelled back.

"Oh, never mind," Bo responded quietly. He stared the ceramic wolf in the eyes for a few more seconds and then gasped loudly.

"Wait! Oh my god!" Bo yelled even louder.

"What? What?"

"No, no, it's stupid, it's stupid." Ed heaved himself up with a sigh and walked over to Bo, sitting down next to him.

"What is it?" he asked, looking at Bo with exasperation.

"I'm like thirty percent sure the wolf moved."

"That's ridiculous."

"Just watch."

Ed sighed an even heavier sigh, if that could be considered possible. He couldn't believe the crazy shit Bo saw sometimes when he got high—but then Ed made eye contact with the wolf as well and could not look away. Six minutes later, both the boys jumped back, and then looked at each other in surprise.

"Did you see it?!" Bo screamed.

"I think so!" Ed responded. "We should probably keep watching just to make sure, though."

"Alright, alright, alright."

They settled back down, sitting cross-legged, and watched the wolf look back at them. This was how Rosalie found them forty-five minutes later when she came to pick them up for their meeting—still dirty, still smelly, and staring at a ceramic wolf in the eyes.

"What are . . . you . . . " Rosalie began to ask.

"Shhhhhh," Ed quieted her. "This is important." Rosalie nodded, unsure, but not in a position to argue. Perhaps this would help crack the case of Ed and Bo, even just a little. She settled down next to them, staring at Ed and Bo, and then eventually making eye contact with the wolf as well. This was how they all sat for the next twelve minutes, in complete and utter silence. Was it weird? Was it bizarre? Was the white and gold tile floor not very comfortable at all? "Yes," would be the answer to all of those questions. But it still happened. As they stared, Ed ignited another one of the CotLaw joints. He took a deep inhale and passed it to Bo, who inhaled as well. He passed it to Rosalie, who hesitated for a long moment. She looked at the wolf, the boys and the joint, and finally took the joint from Bo's hand. She grabbed a long, luxurious drag, gracefully emitting a steady stream of smoke. Ed and Bo would have been mesmerized had they not already been in the process of being mesmerized by the wolf.

The three sat and passed the joint back and forth.

"Do you see it?" Bo asked Rosalie. She shook her head in confusion.

"You have to look. *Really* look," Ed advised. Rosalie set down her notepad, scooted closer, and took another hit. A few moments later, they all breathed out in wonder.

"I see it," Rosalie whispered. They continued to sit and look for quite a few moments. When they collectively came to, they were all holding hands. Rosalie quickly jumped up, smoothing out her shirt.

"It's time to meet Mr. Savage!" she exclaimed as she looked at her watch. "Shit. We're late. Alright. Let's go," she sputtered. Ed and Bo marveled at the alarming break in Rosalie's pristine cool, but just as quickly as it came, it was gone. Rosalie looked them both in the eyes, and the fire came back. The look sent shivers down both of the boys' spines, and suddenly, they were right back in the business trip. The spell of the wolf had been broken, and in its wake, Rosalie's eye contact seemed to have an even stronger effect.

"You boys look great." She beckoned for them to follow her and the boys bounded out after her.

All three of them piled into the elevator, Ed trying not to look at Rosalie and Bo also trying not to look at Rosalie and neither of them succeeding. Rosalie kept her eyes firmly affixed on her notepad and phone, only looking up when the elevator opened. "Boys," she said with a laugh when she caught them both staring at her. They quickly averted their eyes. "You ready to talk business?"

"Always," Ed said.

"Sometimes," Bo corrected. Ed shot him a look.

"What? I mean, like sometimes when we just wake up we aren't ready, ya know? I'm just trying to be honest!" He looked at Rosalie for validation, but she was already out on the street, climbing into the waiting limo. They piled into the car and drove off into the night once more.

7

"**W**elcome to CotLaw Incorporated," Rosalie announced as they walked toward the expansive glass doors. "Cotlaw also owns this," she said with a wry smile. Ed and Bo marveled at the entirely glass structure, which looked kind of like when cities exist in space in movies, except with white and gold trim, and also this wasn't space. The doors opened without a touch and led the three into a warm and welcoming open room. The dark wooden floor was covered with all kinds of interesting graffiti and artwork, from a maroon llama and a sky-blue alpaca sitting in the grass together to a city filled with trees instead of skyscrapers. Bo's eyes were immediately drawn down to the animals and the bizarre illustrations, and he could not tear his eyes away.

"Dude. It's like in my dreams," he whispered to Ed. Ed nodded, mesmerized by the legions of casually dressed young women and men in the room. They congregated around a competitive Ping-Pong match, they sat in beanbag chairs and played video games, and they chatted at the kitchenette. They were all tanned, fit, and apparently incredibly happy.

"Who are these people," Ed breathed out in awe. "And what are they doing?" Rosalie followed his gaze and laughed a bit.

"Oh, these guys? They're working."

Ed and Bo nodded, exhilarated by the designation of this as "working." It may have been close to midnight, but these people were acting as if it was mid-day at an arcade. Ed grinned at Bo and Bo grinned even wider back.

"We don't really keep traditional office hours at

CotLaw. And, we like our employees to be happy, because that's where innovation comes from," Rosalie said pleasantly. She let Ed and Bo stare at them for a few more moments, before continuing. "Go ahead, you can talk to them. They won't bite."

Ed looked nervously back at Rosalie, and she ushered him forward. Bo shrugged and walked up to the closest employee, a blonde woman who looked like she could work in a bike shop.

"Excuse me," Bo said. "What's it like to work for CotLaw?" The woman turned around from the Ping-Pong match to face Bo, smiling as she turned.

"It's incredible. Hi! I'm Eloise," she said, eyes fluttering ever so briefly to Rosalie behind him.

"Bo."

"Bo . . . from Square One?" she said, excitement gathering in her voice.

"Uh, yeah, I guess I am from Square One," he said, looking around for Ed, who had gathered the courage to join them.

"Wow, it's a real pleasure," she said sincerely,

shaking Bo's hand and sighting Ed, hanging back just a few feet. "And you must be Ed!"

He nodded, grinning. Eloise continued with a loud laugh. "It is true what they said! Wow, good job, Rosalie." With that, she was gone, back to the match. Ed and Bo stood, a bit dumbfounded by the whole experience.

"What's true?" Ed asked Bo.

"I'm not exactly sure," Bo answered.

"It's true that you two are just as handsome as she'd been told," Rosalie said with a grin, which of course, returned them to the whole shivers-down-the-spine issue. "No need to be embarrassed boys. If you work with CotLaw, you'll be known. You'll be important. They'll help make that happen."

Ed and Bo nodded, excited by those prospects, but also inching toward the little kitchen filled with an entire array of snack options. The intoxicating smell of free food wafted toward the boys, and Rosalie saw them salivating just a bit.

"Go ahead, it's our complimentary snack service.

Today's theme is peanut butter." That was all the permission Ed and Bo needed, and then they were gone to a better place. It was stocked with all things peanut butter—from a jar of the natural-pressed stuff all the way to peanut butter ice cream sandwiches. Ed and Bo grabbed as much as they could in a pure peanut butter frenzy.

"Dude," Bo said to Ed under his breath.

"I know," Ed responded.

"This is what Square One should be like! This is what it *can* be like," Bo said.

"Super successful and filled with productive people?" Ed asked.

"No, well, I mean, that too, but also super chill and filled with snacks and video games and cool people. Just like our business manifesto said!" Bo exclaimed. But Ed did not have a chance to respond because Rosalie had taken off down a hallway, gesturing for them to follow her.

"Walk and talk, boys," she said, and eyed saw the armfuls of food they were handling. "And eat."

They nodded and began to quickly make their way through their snacks, doing their best not to choke as they toured the headquarters and struggling with the stickiness of the peanut butter on the roof of their mouths.

"Here is our development center," Rosalie said, gesturing to a group of young adults sitting on the floor without their shoes and meditating to the sounds of a rare bird chirping. "And here is the research center," she said, pointing out a room on the left that, again, contained the exact same kind of people laying on massage chairs and getting worked on by overweight masseuses. "Our product testing center," she pointed to yet another room, filled with a group of workers playing the Badge of Honor game and eating popcorn. Ed stopped for just a few minutes at this room to gaze longingly at the advanced multi-player options, before rushing back to catch up with Rosalie and Bo.

They continued to make their way through the

maze of hallways, observing room after room of happy people doing happy things. With each step, Ed and Bo couldn't help but imagine themselves in those rooms, winning Ping-Pong tournaments or eating peanut butter constantly. If this was what being an adult was all about, perhaps it wasn't all that hard. Plus, adults got to hang out with people like Rosalie. Being an adult seemed awesome, and being an adult at CotLaw seemed even more awesome. This was the kind of work environment they were born to be in.

They made their way to an elevator, which brought them from the ground floor past sixteen other floors, and all the way to the penthouse. Rosalie stopped them outside the door and looked at both of them in the eyes.

"Just relax, and get ready for the big meeting."

"It's time?" Ed asked, a bit panicked.

"Don't worry," she said as her voice dropped into a lower octave. "You guys will do great."

Ed and Bo nodded, because they believed her. It

was finally time to meet the boss, *the* Mr. Savage. They had lost a consultation with Mr. Savage to Cameron Walcot all those months ago, but now they were here to meet with him as prospective partners, and they were as terrified as they were thrilled. They took deep breaths, and Ed smoothed out his crinkled t-shirt. Bo took a look at his own t-shirt, which now had a lot of peanut butter stains in addition to the multitude of bloodstains, and made a mental note to get some new clothes tomorrow. They followed Rosalie through the door and into a simple office.

In complete contrast to the rest of the CotLaw building, this room was sparse and traditional. A brown desk with a black chair stood in the center of the room, and nothing else occupied the room besides three chairs across from the table. Even though the room was lackluster, Ed and Bo gasped when they walked in, but only because sitting at the desk was someone whom they had by now forgotten all about.

"Hi, Ed, Bo," Paolo said to them. He leaned back with his feet up on the desk. The nameplate in front of him read: "Mr. Savage."

Ed and Bo stared back at Paolo, both a bit dumbfounded. Honestly, they were getting kind of tired of being dumbfounded all the time; it took a lot out of them. Paolo saw their confused and somewhat alarmed expressions.

"Oh no, I'm not—No, it's not me," Paolo said quickly. "Though I can see how it would look like that. Mr. Savage's desk is just really comfortable."

Rosalie glared at him, but Paolo ignored her and gestured to the chairs.

"Do not sit down, because Mr. Savage could not make it tonight, unfortunately."

"Oh," Bo said, a little crestfallen after the whole buildup.

"Man," Ed muttered. He had been looking forward to meeting the famed business mogul in the flesh.

"Family emergency. Something about a cat.

But don't worry, we have an entire week to meet Mr. Savage. I trust Rosalie has been treating you . . . well?" Paolo said, eyes fluttering between Rosalie and the boys. Both Ed and Bo nodded vehemently in agreement. Paolo smiled widely. "Excellent."

Paolo looked to Rosalie, whose face was flushed. Paolo stared at her, but she looked down at the ground. Ed and Bo had never known Rosalie to not make eye contact. "Why don't you take these kind gentlemen to the special surprise place? I think they'll really enjoy it," Paolo said pointedly. Rosalie nodded, leaving and gesturing for the boys to come. Ed stopped as they were leaving and looked back at Paolo, who had returned back to his paperwork.

"I hope his cat is okay," Ed said with sincerity.

"I'll tell him you said that," Paolo answered whole-heartedly. The boys walked to the elevator behind Rosalie, and at Bo's questioning look, Ed snapped somewhat defensively.

"What? Dude, imagine if I lost Albert . . . I know what that pain is like." Bo thought about losing Albert, and couldn't help but feel a tiny bit relieved, because then he would sneeze a little less in Ed's house.

By the time they had gotten off the elevator, both boys had forgotten about the secret surprise place. Ed was deep in somber contemplation about what it would be like to have to live without Albert, picturing all the major holidays without him. How would he have Thanksgiving dinner without Albert under the couch somewhere? How could he even think about Christmas without little Albert eating the wrapping paper when they were looking away? He didn't even want to start thinking about National Peanut Butter Lovers' Day, let alone the yearly 4/20 celebrations.

Bo was really deeply engrossed in the mechanics behind sneezing and marveling at how weird it was that particles of liquid came out of your nose. What made someone allergic to something?

Why is sneezing the appropriate response? How do allergy medicines work? These questions and more swirled around Bo's mind, so once again, they were completely oblivious when Rosalie stopped in presentation of what was before her.

Neither of them had realized that they had descended to a level titled, "P." In a normal building, this would probably mean parking. But at CotLaw, this "P" meant pool. In front of the boys was an enormous water park, the kind that has a lazy river, a whirlpool, and big slides, but this particular park didn't have any of the annoying attendants telling swimmers not to do stuff. Complete and total pool independence was possible here.

"This is just like . . . " Ed said in a daze.

"Almost an exact replica . . . " Bo muttered.

"Of the waterpark you boys got kicked out of in sixth grade because you both tried to pretend a chocolate bar was a piece of poop?" Rosalie finished the sentence for them.

"Yeah," Ed breathed out.

"Yeah," Bo said. "The best waterpark we never got to enjoy."

Rosalie watched the boys marvel at the pool and couldn't help but smile along with them. She led the boys over to lockers that were labeled with each of their names.

"Paolo left some suits here," Rosalie said with a flourish. They hurried to their lockers and pulled out identical trunks, but the third locker stopped them both.

"This one has your name on it, Rosalie," Bo said as he pointed. Rosalie went over to the locker labeled "Rose," and pulled out a bikini that looked more suitable for a small toddler or Tarzan than a full-grown woman. She pulled off a note and read, "Make sure you take care of them. – P." A visible look of discomfort washed over her face and the deep flush returned.

"Can you boys promise me something?" Rosalie asked in a low tone they had never heard before.

"Yeah," came Ed's soft reply.

"Sure," Bo said.

"Please, be careful here," Rosalie said quietly. The boys looked back at her, more than a little perplexed.

"But we know how to swim," Bo said with a smile.

"Yeah, don't worry. I used to be on the swim team," Ed said proudly. Rosalie opened her mouth to say something else, but before she could, the boys ran and jumped in the pool in their clothes just to prove exactly how well they could swim. Rosalie smiled in spite of herself. Her small smile quickly grew into a loud yell when the boys got out of the pool and rushed toward her.

"No, no, no, no way!" She shouted as the boys picked her up and threw her into the pool, clad fully in her business attire. They screamed and splashed and yelled and enjoyed the waterpark like they wished they could have in sixth grade, thoughts of caution, Paolo, and Mr. Savage pushed to the back of their minds.

Ed and Bo returned to the hotel room in big fluffy white-and-gold robes after they had exhausted themselves at the pool. It had been a long day, and it was crazy to think that they had been in Portland in Ed's garage just that morning. They came into the room and almost immediately collapsed onto the couch, but only after stopping to say hello to the wolf on the way in. Ed and Bo were completely and utterly exhausted, but also incredibly awed by CotLaw.

"Yo. That water felt—"Bo began.

"Like we were moving through time and space. I know."

"I can't believe they have a pool in their office building."

"I can't believe any of this," Ed said. Bo laughed along with him, but then stopped suddenly.

"No, really. Doesn't this all seem just too good to be true? It's very literally everything we like and everything we ever dreamed of," Bo said tentatively. Ed looked back at Bo, a little unsure. But then Ed thought about how cool Paolo was and how beautiful Rosalie was and how awesome CotLaw was and soon enough Bo remembered that too.

"Never mind, I'm just being paranoid," Bo admitted. "Next thing you know, I'm gonna be saying the wolf is talking or something," he said with a smile.

"What?" Ed said, confused until he noticed Bo's secret smile. "Oh, you jackass!" Bo laughed as Ed jumped up and started to punch him mockingly.

"No, he was talking to me! He just told me he'd never talk to you!"

They laughed and fought some more. When their giggles had been fully expended, they retreated to the closest bedroom—they were too exhausted to even deal with sleeping in different beds. Ed fell face down and with his robe still on; Bo kind of made it into boxers before climbing under the covers and quickly nearing sleep.

"Hey, Ed?" Bo asked as his eyes crossed.

"Yeah, Bo?" Ed responded.

"We have gotta call Natalie tomorrow."

"Totally. Tomorrow."

They quickly fell into what may have been the best sleep either of them had ever had. Though to be fair, they usually just slept on Ed's couch at odd hours of the night so it was a pretty low bar to reach. For the first time in a while, neither of them dreamed.

It had only been a day in California, but it had felt like a week to the exhausted minds behind Square One. So, it only made sense that the next six days felt like six additional weeks, especially to those continuously brain-addled minds. Wednesday began with a surfing trip to the beach. Ed and Bo were equally as mesmerized by the concept of a warm beach; coming from Oregon, they didn't exactly have the warmest water to hang out in. Surfing didn't work as well as expected, however. Bo's meager skills on the skateboard did not translate too well to water-skateboarding and Ed didn't really like to take his shirt off outside. They ended up playing in the sand and building some pretty kick-ass sand castles. Rosalie supervised them in her very fashionable, old-school, one-piece swimsuit and an oversized hat. Behind her big, face-obscuring glasses, Rosalie continued to look at that legal pad of hers, though when Ed and Bo started a water gun fight, she couldn't help but join in.

They recovered from some intense sunburn the next day by spending an entire day at the spa. Ed and Bo had never really understood what a spa was, let alone been inside one. They marveled over the cucumber eyes, the Jacuzzi spas, the cold baths, and the hot-stone saunas. It turned out to be not too great for the horrific sunburns they had both acquired, so Ed ended up playing video games in the relaxation room for most of the day, because like any good spa, this one came equipped with video games. Bo watched him play until Rosalie asked to join in, and then Bo couldn't stay away either.

Friday was filled with hiking and nature trail walking, which took a sharp turn when Ed and Bo got incredibly winded from walking up a hill. They struggled on for a bit, still vaguely trying to impress Rosalie. But when all three of them were profusely sweating and looked far too pale, Rosalie called the limo and they drove back down the mountain to a restaurant where they made their own salt and vinegar chips in-house. Ed and Bo and Rosalie began to find a weird kind of connection between the three of them, which made for some great meals and fun days. Rosalie stopped taking out her notepad every time they interacted, and Ed and Bo began to like her more and more, but in a different kind of way. Kind of like the way that they wanted her to give a speech at their future wedding, but not in the way that they wanted her to be the one they married. They started spending long dinners giggling together and talking about themselves and really getting to know one another. Talk about business, CotLaw, and their future faded into the background as discussions of the zombie apocalypse, Velocidactyls, and the weirdest sex dreams they'd ever had became far more enthralling.

The rest of the days seemed to blur by, filled with events like bowling, amusement park going, and concert watching. The earlier tension of the trip faded away into comfortable peace, and each of them genuinely enjoyed spending the days together. Just as Ed and Bo had fallen in love with Rosalie together, they fell into an amicable friendship with her together. Ed and Bo always retreated to the comfort of their suite at night, where they relaxed with a smoke and a discussion about life's greatest mysteries, like where the movie set for the moon-landing faking would have been, assuming that the moon landing was fake. That was something that Bo always assumed and Ed skeptically denied.

But throughout the entire business trip, there was never a meeting with Mr. Savage. They did activities in and around the CotLaw building and always planned to meet up with the man, the myth, the business legend—but each and every time he did not show. At CotLaw's weekly ice cream social Mr. Savage was nowhere to be found. When Rosalie took Ed and Bo to a fancy dinner, the kind that they have to keep their elbows off the table for, Mr. Savage canceled at the last minute. He was always just around the corner in another meeting or just out of reach on an important task. Ed and Bo barely noticed, however, because they were far more interested in the cool stuff they were doing and the constant access to delicious food that CotLaw provided. But before they knew it, the seventh and final day of the trip had come and gone and it was time for the boys to head back home.

8

Ed and Bo sat in the back of the limo with Rosalie and Paolo on the way to the airport, or more accurately, the plot of private land where CotLaw's private plane took off and landed. They were both in low spirits for the first time in a long while. Sure, they generally lived a happy life. Ed got fed three meals a day and Bo often got fed five to six because he ate at Ed's house so often. Ed had a cat he loved and a sister he hated and a mom he was okay with. Bo had mystery parents that Ed was really starting to suspect worked for the CIA. They had each other and a solid place to chill and legs they could walk around on. They were owners of a locally successful business. Sure, all of this was true—but nothing in their old life was at all like living in California with CotLaw. These were adults who had figured out how to make money by being kids, which could quite possibly be the absolute perfect place for two chill dudes like Ed and Bo. The boys knew that this was the kind of work environment Square One was destined to have, and it was incredible to be able to see their future in action.

They had both done some serious thinking about their future while gallivanting around town. Ed had pictured himself as a business mogul with legions of happy, attractive, and talented workers. Bo had imagined getting a little dog that he could carry around everywhere, because everyone had dogs out here. Eventually, the dog would embody the spirit of the wolf in the hotel and he would have a really cool pet. In short, both of them loved the whole "Silicon Valley" thing and suddenly the future seemed a lot less scary.

Ed and Bo sat in deep, mutual thought, partially reflecting on the past week but mostly just not wanting to leave. As they neared the plane, Rosalie started to look a little bit sadder while Paolo retained his impassively gray gaze. Before anybody could stop it, the limo pulled up alongside the tiny CotLaw plane.

"Here we are," Paolo said warmly. "Your plane, boys." He jumped out and opened the door for Ed and Bo. They sat for just a few moments longer with Rosalie. She looked them both in the eyes. The fire was gone, and in its place was an entirely different kind of warmth.

"I'm—" Ed stopped and looked at Bo. "We're going to miss you."

Bo nodded vehemently. Rosalie looked back at them with the hint of a smile, eyes twinkling.

"I'm going to miss you too, boys," she said, reaching out for a hug. Ed and Bo both froze in fear, because neither of them ever knew exactly what to do when a woman tried to hug them. Whenever Ed's Aunt Milda tried to hug him at

Christmas, she ended up engulfing him in her massive body and holding onto him for far too long. So, in defense, he usually ended up just standing still with his arms at his side. Last Thanksgiving, Natalie opened the door at the DeLancey's when Bo arrived. She went in for a hug, because this was the kind of dinner with no elbows on the table, and Bo went in far too fast and eagerly, accidentally bumping heads with her. Both boys had both learned from their previous traumas that hugging a woman was dangerous territory indeed, especially with someone as compelling as Rosalie.

So, when Rosalie went in for a hug in the limo, the boys tried to apply what they had learned. Ed went in fast, arms up and away from his side, and Bo sat still and just leaned in slightly. The result was a bizarre mish mash of seated people vaguely touching each other. Rosalie's arms just made it around both boys, Ed bumped into her, and Bo was oddly too far back. No one admitted the moment was awkward because it was also what made it beautiful. Over the boys' heads, Paolo discreetly winked at Rosalie. He mouthed, "Good job," silently as she paled and turned away, burying her face in the hug. Out of the earshot of Paolo, she discreetly whispered to the boys.

"Remember, be careful."

Then she pulled away and turned immediately back toward the car. Ed and Bo quickly left as well, now a little bit embarrassed by the sincerity. They waved goodbye to Rosalie sitting in the car behind them. Paolo threw the boys' bags to them as they walked toward the plane. Right as they neared the stairs to the plane, Madison and Liz came out to beckon them aboard. Paolo stopped and turned to face the two boys, putting his hand firmly on first Ed's shoulder, and then Bo's.

"This is where I leave you, boys. I've got to stay to attend to some important business over here." Ed and Bo nodded.

"Now, in terms of contracts," Paolo began, and

then stopped himself. "You know, don't worry about it."

"What?" Ed asked with excitement.

"It's alright, we can talk later. You're tired," Paolo insisted.

"Tell us!" Bo said.

Paolo shrugged and leaned in. "Alright. I can give you guys this contract, but I need to know if you're in or not first."

Without looking at each other, Ed and Bo both nodded in unison.

"Of course," Ed said.

"We're so in," Bo reiterated. They stood looking at Paolo with wide eyes, and he smiled.

"Glad to hear it, boys," he said. He pulled out a sizable stack of papers. "Here's the contract. Let's have that signed by next week when I'm back in town, alright?"

Ed and Bo nodded eagerly once more.

"Oh, and one more thing," Paolo continued. "The partnership price. Ten thousand dollars."

"Excuse me?" Bo coughed.

"How are we supposed to get that kind of money together?" Ed exclaimed. Paolo just smiled and shook his head. He leaned in close and put both of his arms around their shoulders, turning them and walking toward the plane.

"No, my boys, *we* pay *you* ten thousand dollars." He walked them up to the stairs and gently pushed them forward. They both looked back, now even more disoriented than before.

"I'll see you on Tuesday! Let's say . . . four p.m.? I'll send the car." Ed and Bo halfheartedly tried to respond, but Paolo was gone into the limo, which was speeding off back to the city. Madison and Liz escorted the boys to their seats and gave them both ginger ales and chips, asking if they needed anything else. Both of them murmured "no" and "thank you" but were still pretty focused on that whole ten-thousand-dollar thing.

"Dude," Bo began. "We could live off of ten

thousand dollars for like, for like, at least thirty years."

"I know," Ed answered, marveling at their fortune.

"We could pay someone to make a Velocidactyl," Bo said.

"We could get a house and a car probably," Ed answered.

"We could move to California and work with CotLaw full time," Bo offered.

"And see Rosalie."

"And see Rosalie," Bo affirmed. They high fived, which inadvertently made the video game screens descend down from the ceilings. Ed and Bo chuckled and high fived again, which brought out their controllers.

"Hey, Ed?" Bo asked.

"Yeah, Bo?"

"Why do you think she told us to be careful again?"

"She probably just meant in the flight."

"Oh. Yeah. Probably."

They began to play Badge of Honor as the plane took off and headed back to Portland, but their minds were still firmly entrenched in California.

An hour and a half later, Ed and Bo were back on Portland soil and strangely happy to see their old familiar sights. Naturally, a limo was waiting at the landing strip to take Ed and Bo back to their garage, but of course, this one did not have Rosalie inside it. As they neared Ed's garage, they sat in contemplative silence. They had spent an entire week yelling and laughing and joking, and now it seemed to be the time for quiet reflection on the imminent acquisition of ten thousand dollars. However, the time for quiet reflection abruptly ended when they pulled alongside the house and Terry appeared out of nowhere. She tapped on the window vehemently, making both Ed and Bo jump. They slowly rolled down the window.

"Where. The. Hell. Have. You. Idiots. Been?" Terry spat out at them, quite literally. Ed and Bo wiped the spit off of their face and remembered they had never exactly remembered to call Natalie.

"Uh . . . we got abducted . . . " Bo said lamely.

Terry rolled her eyes and shouted, "Abducted!" She laughed and shook her head before getting back on her bike and speeding down off into the night. Ed and Bo reluctantly got out of the limo and shuffled slowly up the driveway and into the light streaming out of the garage.

"She's going to kill us," Bo said weakly.

"I bet it's in shambles," Ed bemoaned. "We never should have left her in charge. So stupid."

"So stupid," Bo agreed. They walked up the driveway into what they were sure would be utter chaos, only to find a row of unfamiliar workers sitting behind a row of desks and phones.

"Hello, thank you for calling Square One, what do you want?"

"Hello, thank you for calling Square One, what do you want?"

"Hello, thank you for calling Square One, what do you want?"

Alexandra strode from the kitchen out to her bike, jumping on and pedaling past Ed and Bo without a second look.

"Natalie, I'm headed on a two-twelve!" she shouted behind her.

"Copy that," came that familiar voice from the back. Bo's heart dropped and Ed shook his head in disbelief. Natalie stood in the back in front of a wall of whiteboards filled with complex codes and schedules and routes. She finished writing *212— Baked Good to West Side* under Alexandra's name and then turned around to face Ed and Bo. Her smile immediately fell into one of the most extreme grimaces of displeasure.

"Welcome home, assholes." Ed and Bo looked at each other, and said the only thing they could think of.

"Hi," Bo said.

"Hello," Ed offered.

The three of them stood in stony silence as the sounds of the phones ringing ricocheted through the garage. The door from the kitchen opened once more and Hoodie Joseph stuck his head out into the garage.

"Natalie, I'm all done with the gluten-free cupcake-brownie—oh." He stopped abruptly when he saw the boys before him. "You're back. Super." Hoodie Joseph turned around and headed back into the kitchen without another word.

"We need to talk," Natalie declared. "But first, get off your asses and help us out, why don't you?" She threw two bike helmets to the boys. They reluctantly strapped the helmets to their heads, because neither of them were in a place to argue with Natalie's fury right now.

Hours later, Ed, Bo, and Natalie sat on the old familiar couch, exhausted in the old familiar way.

"—And it was just so fast and so sudden, we didn't really even have time," Bo said anxiously.

"We really tried to call like two or three or six times, but we couldn't get through," Ed added.

"And we were so busy with all this business stuff," Bo continued.

"We just really couldn't call," Ed finished.

Natalie stared back at them impassively. "Bullshit," she declared, with a force that neither of them had exactly heard in her before. "Tell me the truth."

Ed and Bo looked at each other.

"We forgot," Bo said.

"We're sorry," Ed added.

Natalie considered both of them for a long while, before shaking her head and muttering, "I hired six new employees. We're making two and a half times the profit. The average delivery is six minutes faster now. So," she concluded. "You have to pay me now. A lot. That's the only way I'll forgive you guys."

Ed stared at her with narrowed eyes and Bo leaned over to him. They consulted for a few brief moments before breaking apart and looking back at Natalie.

"Alright," Ed assented. "Deal."

All three of them shook on it. Natalie bounded up and headed to the kitchen door as fast as she could.

"I'm still mad, though," she yelled back as she headed out. "And also I'm dating Cameron!"

Ed and Bo were left staring dumbstruck after the little sister who had become a cunning negotiator in just a week's time. They looked at each other, and did the only thing they could at a time like this. They curled up on the couch and fell into a deep sleep.

The next morning, Ms. DeLancey prepared an amazing "Welcome Home, Businessmen" breakfast. Eggs, bacon, and pancakes were not even all that bad when they came from a can. Ed and Bo had sorely missed the deliciousness of their elaborate weekend breakfasts. Albert the cat sat in Ed's lap for most of the meal, treasuring the return of his only male ally in the house. They ate and told the DeLanceys the stories of their trip. Ms. DeLancey and Natalie "ooh"ed and "aah"ed at all the fun things they did, but Natalie asked one very important question.

"When did you guys do business stuff?" she asked. Bo laughed and Ed scoffed at her.

"Natalie, Natalie, Natalie," Ed began. "The point is that it was all business stuff."

"It sounds like it was all just eating and going to amusement parks."

"It was called a SkateCade, Natalie. Help me out, Bo."

Bo thought for a bit and shrugged.

"Yeah, no, we did business like the whole time. I think," Bo said.

Natalie smiled and went back to her eggs.

"If you say so."

They returned to eating, although Ed and Bo

had a little bit more to think about now. Soon enough a familiar bickering match erupted between Ed and Natalie, and Ms. DeLancey leaned over to Bo and began to whisper furtively.

"Natalie says she got a call from an old-sounding man who wanted more of the same 'treasured advice' you had given him?" She leaned in as she spoke, lifting her eyebrows as she said, "treasured."

"Oh, yeah! Old Hunchback! Man, probably needs help with an iPad or something."

"Is that the man in the mansion over on Grosvenor?" Ms. DeLancey continued, forcibly keeping her voice light.

"Yeah, he had this whole weird thing about maps and conspiracies and stuff."

"What kind of conspiracies?"

At this, Bo paused, remembering he had sworn himself to secrecy. "I, uh, I can't really say, Ms. DeLancey. You know, Square One rules."

"Come on, Bo, you can tell me!" she said with a warm smile.

"Why does it matter?" he asked with suspicion.

"Oh, it's just, uh, related to my scrapbooking project. I'm scrapbooking about . . . big houses like his," she said, not at all convincingly. Bo shrugged and shook his head once more.

"I can't, Ms. DeLancey, sorry," he affirmed. Ms. DeLancey studied his eyes briefly before nodding and leaning back into her chair, resuming her same old smile. Bo briefly considered the possibility that something bigger was happening in his town than he ever could have imagined, but then quickly realized this was probably just another one of his crazy theories. When Ms. DeLancey insisted they all take seconds and everyone chattered happily once more, Bo decided it was definitely just one of his crazy theories.

9

"**I don't know why you would think it's a** good idea to come here," Bo spat out at Ed through the dull roar of hipsters drinking lattes. "You *know* I prefer to ingest my caffeine in soda or chocolate form."

"It's time to grow up a little, man. Today is the day we become official CotLaw business partners. We gotta start drinking coffee." Ed took a tentative sip of the concoction he had ordered, termed a "Dirty Sally." He grimaced when he tasted the bitter snap of the espresso and the overpowering dark roast that came off as more of a sensory attack than a drink he would enjoy in the morning. Bo watched him closely, and so Ed forced a smile. "Mmmm. Delicious."

"Bullshit," Bo said as he took a sip of his hot chocolate with extra whipped cream. They sat in the RedElephant, one of seven nearly identical, locally sourced, fair-trade coffee shops that roasted their own beans on site. The store was lined from wall to wall with various tattooed individuals; probably about sixty percent of the room wore trendy hats, and the rest wore large-framed glasses. Everyone sat brooding by themselves in a corner, working on their screenplays, theses, or Portland treasure conspiracy theories as the case may be. Ed and Bo were just dirty enough to not stick out too much, and Ed envisioned their future work breakfasts, work meetings, and work ideas happening in adult places like this very RedElephant. Bo just saw some overpriced coffee and a lot of people dressed like they hadn't seen a department store in six years.

"I think we should leave," Bo said as he gulped

down his delicious hot chocolate, determined not to let it go to waste.

"Alright, fine, but all I'm saying is that we're going to need some place other than Al's Diner to take our millionaire business partners to. And especially our billionaire business partners," Ed said as he pushed out his chair and accidentally hit the man sitting behind him.

"Oh, sorry," he said while standing up.

"It's alright," came the robotic reply. Ed and Bo would know that monotone anywhere and Bo couldn't help but exclaim.

"Belfroy?!" He screeched, and then clapped a hand over his mouth because he realized that acknowledging someone meant he had to talk to him. Belfroy turned around with that same grin on his face, but decked out in an outdated beret and a V-neck sweater. He was basically a hipster robot, which is as terrible as it sounds.

"Hello, Ed, Bo," he said curtly, nodding to them. "How's the summer going?"

"Um, good, I guess," Ed stammered. An awkward silence fell between them as they fumbled to find the right way to talk to each other in a non-guidance room setting.

"Gearing up for college in the fall?" Belfroy asked. The question hung like a black cloud in the air. Ed and Bo were well aware that you should never tell your guidance counselor you're not going to college, but they really saw no way out.

"I think we're gonna go corporate, actually," Bo said when the silence had gotten to be too much.

"It's really great, we got this whole business deal figured out and everything. We're going to be rich and probably maybe famous without even having to go to school," Ed said, gaining steam. For the very first time in their four years of knowing Belfroy, his grin turned down ever so slightly.

"I'm sorry to hear that," he said, an audible crack in his monotone creeping into his voice.

"No, really!" Bo assured him. "It's amazing! There's so much peanut butter and people playing video games all day and all the kinds of food you could want and Rosalie and a lot of money!"

Ed and Bo stood across from hipster Belfroy, unsure why they felt the need to explain themselves to a man who now had no bearing on their future whatsoever.

"Just promise me this, Ed and Bo," he said as he leaned forward. "Read the contract. And think about school. You both have some good options and it'd be a shame to waste them." With that, Belfroy got up and headed past the boys, clapping them each firmly on the shoulder as he went. They watched him leave, feeling strangely like they were getting broken up with. As Belfroy reached the door, he turned around and looked back. "And remember, hang in there."

"Dude. We can't let the words of Belfroy, of all people, sway our decision," Ed said through a mouth full of yogurt. "Which I didn't even really think was a decision. Obviously we're going to take the money."

Bo sat on the couch next to him, unconvinced.

"I'm not saying we shouldn't take the money, I'm just saying . . . I don't know exactly . . . but it was all kind of spooky, ya know?"

"Well, obviously it was spooky. He's a robot," Ed said casually. Bo turned to face him, watching Ed closely as he took another spoonful of yogurt. Ed squirmed a bit and punched him weakly.

"What are you doing, man?" Ed asked.

"This is the very first time you've admitted that Belfroy is a robot. I just want to remember it," Bo said dreamily. Ed shoved him a little.

"Stop being an idiot. We're signing the contract."

Bo shrugged noncommittally and Ed continued, "Belfroy doesn't even know what he's talking about. Even if we wanted to go to school, it's too late now."

Bo shrugged again. "Just, like, what are the details? Are we just gonna close down here and

move shop entirely? What about our customers?"
Ed just spooned more yogurt into his mouth.

"I don't know, man, it's probably in that thing somewhere," he said, vaguely gesturing to the thick contract they couldn't bring themselves to open. "They'll definitely go over it in the meeting."

"The meeting! Isn't that soon?" Bo said, sitting up a bit.

"Shit. Yeah. What time is it?!" Ed squeaked, dropping his yogurt with a thud.

"Three forty-three."

"Yeah, the meeting is in seventeen minutes."

"We gotta get ready!"

"I'll get the weed."

"Aren't we out?"

"Oh. Shit."

They sat in silent desperation for a few moments before another pressing issue came to Ed.

"What does one wear when one becomes a billionaire?" Ed asked. Bo thought for a while and answered thoughtfully, "Well, the richest guy I can think of is that Facebook guy."

Ed nodded and smiled—that could be arranged. A few searches through the closet later, Ed and Bo both donned the soft-as-clouds On The House hoodies that Cameron had given them, which were the only hoodies they owned, much to Bo's chagrin. They rounded out the look with old jeans and tattered sneakers. They were ready to make the deal that would make them a billion or a million or a thousand dollars or something. Ed peered anxiously out the window. No limo yet. Bo paced rapidly in the garage, wishing they could smoke. They were both tense with the anticipation of the rest of their lives ahead of them, which seemed to be controlled by this single upcoming moment.

Ed thought about making billions and being the richest eighteen-year-old there ever was and then finally having sex with Hayley Plotinsky, once he had enough money to make her want to hang out with him. He smiled a little bit, and then an important eighteenth birthday-related memory came to him. He opened up the side couch cushion to pull out some of the emergency stash they'd left behind from that night.

"Oh shit! I forgot about that!" Bo exclaimed. Ed smiled slyly.

"Shall we?"

Bo nodded vehemently. Ed began to parcel it out and prepared to roll, but could not find rolling papers anywhere. Bo jumped up to help and the two tore apart the entire garage, only turning up a dusty bag of salt and vinegar chips that they promptly ate in frustration, a tennis ball, and vintage *Playboys* that Ed had once found at a garage sale. They fell onto the couch and eyed the DinoBong in front of them.

"Dude. We can't," Bo said sadly. "Last time we smoked this with that—"

"I know. My mom still hides some of her globes at night just in case we try to eat them."

"There must be something in here . . . " Bo said, trailing off, because his eyes had landed on the contract. Ed followed his gaze, and shook his head vehemently. Bo nodded just as vehemently.

Contrary to popular opinion, important legal documents make excellent rolling papers. Ed and Bo cackled at their ingenuity as they cut tiny slips of paper out of the document. They used a page hidden deep in the packet, hoping that no one would notice at the meeting. Ed sliced papers of varying sizes and Bo began to roll them up. They smoked one joint, sinking deeper into the couch and feeling much more like classic rich dudes. There was still no sight of the limo when they were done, and Bo humbly suggested another joint. Ed jumped to the contract, cutting out a little rectangle and handing it to Bo. But just as Bo lit up the joint and exhaled a tremendous amount of smoke, Ed let out a noise that sounded like a mouse crying, and turned to Bo.

"Hey, Bo?"

"Yeah, Ed?" He responded, holding back a giggle.

"I think we should maybe read the contract," Ed said solemnly, all traces of hysteria gone. Bo's face immediately fell as he sensed Ed's urgency. "Specifically this part," he said, handing the contract to Bo and pointing to the clause right next to the portion Ed had just cut for their next joint.

CLAUSE SIXTEEN

Whereas the co-owners of "Square One," upon signing the document and upon receipt of their payment of ten thousand dollars, forfeit any and all rights of ownership to the business. All future activities of Square One will be overseen and decided by CotLaw Corporation. This is a complete forfeit of rights. See Clause Nineteen.

"Shit," Bo said simply. "Maybe it's a mistake?" Ed shook his head and pointed to Clause Nineteen.

CLAUSE NINETEEN: COMPLETE FORFEITURE
OF RIGHTS

*As aforementioned, the co-owners of Square
One forfeit all rights from the point of signing,
for the rest of time. At no point will the co-
owners, or their heirs, or their heirs' heirs, be
entitled to any portion of any future profit. See
Clause Thirty-Eight.*

"Shit," Bo said again, because there was nothing else to say. Ed's face was even paler than usual
and Bo dropped his head into his hands. "But that
doesn't necessarily mean that—" Ed just pointed
to Clause Thirty-Eight.

CLAUSE THIRTY-EIGHT: FORFEITURE OF
INVOLVEMENT IN PRODUCTION

*The co-owners of Square One, Mr. ED
DELANCEY and Mr. BARTOLOMEU "BO"
DAWSON, hereby forfeit any and all future*

involvement with Square One and its associated productions.

Ed turned to Bo and Bo turned to Ed.

"Dude," Ed breathed.

"Dude," Bo answered.

"Your name is Bartolomeu?" Ed asked. Bo shoved him, smiling in spite of himself.

"Our company is crumbling at our fingertips and that's all you can say?"

"No. I can also say that we've been duped."

Bo nodded, solemn once more.

"What's the rest of the contract like?" Bo asked hesitantly. Ed paged through the contract, skimming the words quickly because he didn't really understand them that well.

"Um. A lot of legal words."

"That's how they get us," Bo said, eyes firmly on the ceiling. "They fill this thing with so many legal words there's no way we'd make it to the forfeiting of rights parts."

"I know. I just can't believe that Rosalie didn't figure it out," Ed said. Bo slowly lowered his eyes from the ceiling and looked at Ed, who was feeling the hair on his arm in intense detail.

"Dude. She was a part of it."

"What? No," Ed said quickly.

"Her and Paolo, man. Come on. Think about it. She had to have been in on it."

Ed shook his head vehemently, but then started to think back. He remembered that green legal pad that had appeared at so many different places.

"Paolo found out what *we* liked . . . " Ed began tentatively.

"And then Rosalie sold it to us," Bo declared. He got up and walked around the garage before sitting down in the corner. Their depressed revelry was rudely interrupted by the beep of a limo out front.

"Shit," they both said at the same time, and then acting fast, they both jumped up and ran to the soda shelf, which only had one can of ginger ale left on it. Bo was just barely able to grab it before Ed.

"You owe me a soda," Bo said, grinning, and Ed handed him over a dollar for the soda.

"That's the highest I'll go."

"Works for me," Bo said, pocketing the money. "Now we just need nine thousand, nine hundred, and ninety-nine more and we can walk away from the contract but still get the money."

"Oh yeah. The contract." The limo honked again, but neither Ed nor Bo could go out to the car, not yet.

"We need a plan," Bo said, staring at the legalese in front of them. Ed nodded, and then jumped up and dug through the dusty back of the garage, pulling out the whiteboard that Square One was born on. It still had weird, circled words lining the board, like "business," and "success." Ed tried to erase it, but they had apparently written with permanent marker. Giving up, he just started to write over the existing words. He scrawled in big letters,

"Ed and Bo Fight Back," on top of the board. He numbered one through three on the board.

"Step One," Ed said, and then trailed off as he looked at Bo in question.

"Um," Bo thought. "Get in the limo that's out front." Ed nodded and wrote it down on the board.

"Great work. Step Two. Go to the meeting that the limo is taking us to," Ed continued, writing as he spoke. "Now the hard one. Step Three." Ed looked at Bo and Bo looked at Ed and they both had really no idea how to negotiate a business deal, so they stuck to what they did know.

"We humiliate Paolo," Bo said, a smile starting to creep across his face. The limo honked once more and this time Ed yelled back.

"We're coming!" Then, turning to Bo, he knelt down in front of his face. "I know that look. You have an idea in there. Come on. Let it form. Do it for all the Velocidactyls we will own one day. You got this."

Bo nodded and entered a look of deep

concentration. It was very nearly the same look he wore when he pooped, but with slightly less frowning. Ed sat down on the floor and waited for the inspiration to strike or for Bo to poop, whichever came first. Either way, something exciting was about to happen. Bo's face rotated through concentration to a look of near panic to a deeply infectious smile and back to concentration. His mind raced through the events of the past week, the events of the past year, and the events of the past life. The weed may have been strong but Bo's mind was stronger, because after a solid ten seconds of some of the most intense concentration Bo had ever undertaken, he looked directly into Ed's eyes.

"Get me six pages of paper. Also a computer that can write on those pages."

"So, you mean like a regular computer? And a printer?"

"I'm not trying to tell you how to live, man, I'm just telling you what I need," Bo said, stretching his hands and legs in anticipation of the imminent adventure. Ed rolled his eyes, because Bo liked to talk like a spy a little bit too much sometimes.

"Alright. Let's go to my computer." The boys got up to go inside, and the limo honked once more. Ed opened the garage door a crack and got on the floor and yelled in response, because he had endured enough rudeness for one day. The contract betrayal was quite enough.

"WE WILL BE THERE AS SOON AS WE FIGURE OUT HOW TO DOUBLE-CROSS YOU!" Ed yelled, causing Bo to erupt into chuckles behind him.

"Dude, don't give it away," he said softly, although the limo driver had never been seen and was probably actually a robot. They walked inside to the computer to get revenge in the only way they knew how.

10

Ed and Bo perched in the backseat of the limo, trying to channel the power of the Facebook guy through the hoodies. They definitely felt a little bit mousier, at the very least.

They sat in tense anticipation, each mentally preparing in their own special kind of way. Ed went over the plan again and again in his head, trying to figure out any potential pitfalls or ways that he could mess it up. Bo tried to picture the huge corporate office and how they would have to sneak through lasers and jump over obstacles and maybe save a few lives in the process. The limo started to slow down a bit as it entered through a large gate, and the boys were drawn out of their preparation.

"I think we're ready," Ed said through clenched teeth.

"I don't know how to jump over lasers that well, though," Bo replied, a bit panicked. Ed didn't respond, because he knew that it was often much easier to just let Bo solve these sorts of things in his own mind. The limo slowed down to a stop and Bo pushed aside images of a dragon guarding a castle, because that was probably not going to happen. The two emerged from the limo to face their new arch nemesis: the CotLaw Corporation building, downtown Portland office. More accurately, the people inside it, but the building seemed to stand for a hell of a lot more. They looked at each other, nodded, and walked into the CotLaw office.

Not at all surprisingly, it was nothing like what Bo had imagined in the limo ride. He looked around for lasers or some kind of mystical guard, but was greeted with more of the same white and gold palace they had gotten used to in California. In fact, this building seemed to be almost exactly the same as the California branch, complete with a large open room and a lot of attractive young people playing games. Ed leaned over to whisper to Bo.

"That's how we can tell they're trying to fool us. Nobody works like this outside of Silicon Valley." Bo nodded in response, still searching for some sort of small dragon, at the very least, but not finding any. They walked up to the front desk and a young woman in a blazer and cool glasses greeted them by name.

"Ed! Bo! So glad to see you. Right this way, please." She took off through the maze of people and hallways, winding by the only place worth visiting—the food table.

"Help yourself, please," she said, gesturing to wide array of snacks before her. Ed instinctively flinched toward the food, but something larger stopped him. Bo pulled him back, shaking his head sadly.

"We can't, man. We gotta stick to our morals and our dignities or . . . something . . . " Bo trailed off as he smelled a fresh-out-of-the-oven cinnamon bun, but then shook his head to break himself out of it. "We can't, we can't," Bo continued. Ed nodded sadly, inhaling deeply as he shook his head.

"Just let me have this," Ed said softly.

The two boys stood still for more than a few moments, smelling the smells of freshly baked pastries and thinking about what could have been had they sold their souls. Meanwhile, the receptionist vaguely smiled behind them, shifting from foot to foot a little nervously. Finally their moments were over, and Ed and Bo turned back to the receptionist, nodding. She led them back through the halls once more.

Ed and Bo followed the receptionist back to the elevator, not even having to dodge any lasers. She walked them in and pressed a new button they had never seen in an elevator—"S." She smiled at their confused expressions. "It's Mr. Savage's personal office here. Just go on up and he'll be waiting." Ed gulped, more than a little alarmed.

"Mr. Savage?" He asked.

"*The* Mr. Savage?" Echoed Bo.

The receptionist smiled the same bland, generally pleasing smile. "The very same. He's very excited to meet you both." With that, she closed the elevator door, waving a goodbye. Ed and Bo turned to each other in panic.

"This wasn't part of the plan!" Ed yelled.

"How are we going to trick the smartest businessman in the entire country?" Bo said woefully, wishing that he could have been so lucky as to face mere dragons. The elevator ticked up through the floors, making its way toward the dreaded "S." Ed looked at Bo and Bo looked back and they both did the only thing they could—they shrugged.

"What does Belfroy always say?" Ed said as his eyes began to narrow in determination.

"You're not going to graduate?"

"Besides that."

"Um . . . " Bo thought as the elevator reached the floor right below S. "Hang in there," he said with finality.

"I think that's just what we gotta do," Ed said.

"I can't believe you're quoting Belfroy at a time like this," Bo said.

"Me neither."

The elevator doors opened to floor S, and Ed and Bo fist bumped each other in solidarity, ready to face the CotLaw Corporation. Sitting there, smiling as pleasantly as ever, was Paolo. The office space was the only room devoid of the white and gold—the only room besides Mr. Savage's office in California. Paolo sat behind a sturdy brown desk, the kind that you saw at an antique store for a lot of money. The dark hardwood floors, the real kind of wood, were adorned with simple carpet that read—"S." It was a grand open room, but in contrast to the rest of CotLaw, it did not feel open and welcoming. This room was sparse and overbearing, containing only a desk and a rug in what looked big enough to be a warehouse. Ed and Bo stepped off the elevator and their footsteps echoed throughout the room. In spite of himself, Bo whispered, "Echo" to the room and it reverberated back silently.

The boys had talked about this moment, but they hadn't exactly pictured this moment happening in real life. Ed had been so focused on the plan itself and Bo had been busy concocting guard-dragons, so neither of them exactly knew how to carry themselves in the long walk to the desk. Paolo waved them over with a flip of his hand and the boys embarked on the journey. Ed tried to take on a sort of swagger as he navigated the floor, which ended up looking like a bizarre limp. Bo went for the classic chest-out look, but he couldn't exactly figure out how to arch his back in a masculine way and ended up looking more like a stretching cat. For better or for worse, Ed and Bo limped and cat-walked over to Paolo. They stopped in front of his desk, realizing that Paolo was the only person in the room. Both of them briefly looked around the room, as if Mr. Savage could be hiding behind a curtain, but no signs of life were found. Paolo had his head buried in documents, and Ed and Bo stood at the desk a bit awkwardly. Finally, Paolo looked up.

"Boys," he drawled, gray-eyes blazing. "Welcome to the start of the rest of your lives." He paused dramatically, letting his words sink in. Ed smiled and Bo squinted a bit, finally speaking because the silence felt too uncomfortable.

"Thank you," Bo said in confusion, and Ed nudged him hard in the ribs. Bo flinched and shot Ed an "Ow!" look. Paolo just smiled some more and continued.

"No need to thank me, gentlemen. Please, take a seat." He gestured behind the boys, and Ed started to object about the lack of chairs in the room. But this time Bo nudged him, and behind them were two leather chairs.

"How did . . . " Ed muttered, and then shook his head. He nodded to Bo and they both sat down in unison, subduing the urge to declare a physical jinx. Ed and Bo sat and stared back at Paolo, and it all felt just a little bit too much like déjà vu. But this time, Ed and Bo were dressed like rich tech dudes and they had a plan. No one was going to tell them what to do. No one was going to con them out of anything. They were staying strong and they would be on high alert.

"If I could just have you two start to fill out these forms," Paolo said as he handed them two clipboards with a personal data sheet. Ed had to elbow Bo again a few seconds later, because Bo was filling out the sheet as if nothing was wrong.

"Dude," he whispered to Bo under his breath, gesturing to his sheet. Under "NAME" it read "Mr. Butts." Bo laughed in appreciation before realizing that he had been putting down his real information. He was just about to hit "SOCIAL SECURITY NUMBER," and after thinking for a few moments, put down "Your Mom." He smiled proudly and showed it to Ed, who shrugged. He had seen better. When they were both done with their forms, Ed glanced around the room for Mr. Savage a few more times.

"I'm sorry to be the bearer of bad news, but Mr. Savage will unfortunately not be available today," Paolo said. At this news, Ed threw up his hands and Bo exhaled as if he had been holding his breath this entire time, because he had been. "But he will be Skyping in." Now Bo threw up his hands and Ed exhaled as if he had been holding his breath for five seconds, because he had been. The boys' poor hearts couldn't take this much excitement, and both of them were getting pretty confused as to what their actual plan was with all these twists and turns. Paolo stood up with grandeur.

"I'll go pull out your file and we can make this official," he said, making his way to the very back corner of the room where one single file cabinet was hidden behind a curtain. As soon as Paolo was out of earshot, the boys began furiously whispering to each other, struggling to make sure their voices didn't echo.

"When do we actually do the 'embarrass them' part of the plan?" Bo whispered urgently.

"Um . . . I think . . . I'm not sure. You're the one who thought it up!" Ed whispered back.

"Yeah, but you were supposed to remember it!" Bo said.

"Just because you have the memory of a fish doesn't mean I have to remember everything!" Ed responded.

"That's exactly what it means!"

The boys were now whisper-yelling and glancing repeatedly at Paolo to make sure he hadn't noticed. He was leafing through files in the cabinet and muttering to himself. Ed turned to Bo and grabbed him by the shoulders.

"Look. We don't have much time. If we don't make it out of here alive—" Ed began.

But Bo cut him off. "I know man, I know."

"You know that I'm—"

"Giving me your entire Badge of Honor collection and entrusting me to continue to defend your place as Portland's number seven player? Of course I know that." Bo smiled at Ed reassuringly and they both experienced a very rare but very powerful moment of clarity.

It's an old legend that when two stoners look at each other in the eyes, both searching for the answer to the same thing, something amazing can happen. Some people go their whole lives searching for this moment, but the legend makes it perfectly clear that only those who are unsuspecting and most deserving and, of course, most high are blessed enough to receive such an honor. You may recognize some crucial moments of history from these exact moments—Ben and Jerry putting cookie dough into ice cream, John Crate and Henry Barrel deciding to sell stylish furniture together, whenever Timbaland makes a song with someone else, etc. All these moments were, in fact, inspired by a duo of stoners on an otherworldly journey.

Ed looked into Bo's eyes and Bo looked into Ed's and they both knew what to do. In the meantime, Paolo had found the file and was now sitting in front of them at the desk. Apparently the boys' moment of clarity had turned into several moments of clarity. Paolo presented the contract and an accompanying pen to the boys.

"Just sign this and we'll be well on our way to billions."

"And Mr. Savage?" Ed asked, looking through the document.

"We'll Skype him and he'll give me permission to sign on his behalf," Paolo answered.

"Great." Ed continued to look through the document, before turning to Bo. "Bo, isn't there something you wanted to ask Paolo here?"

Bo nodded confidently, then leaned in close to Paolo.

"I need your help, and it's of a very personal

nature." This finally drew Paolo up from his half-attention, and he leaned in a bit as well. "Please, can we go talk in the corner?" Bo asked furtively. Paolo's eyes widened and he nodded. Bo and Paolo walked over to the file cabinet corner while Ed made the switch. Bo talked to Paolo for a good three minutes, far longer than Ed needed to complete his part of the plan. Bo swung his arms a few times, made the gesture for something big getting smaller, and gestured to his crotch continuously. Paolo's eyes widened and narrowed accordingly and he shook his head sadly, because he simply had no possible advice to offer the poor guy. Bo sighed heavily, and the two came back to the table. Paolo looked a little paler and Bo winked at Ed. Ed handed the paper over to Bo, who signed it without looking. They handed the contract back to Paolo, who was now smiling in a way that suggested he just won a laser-tag game or something equally as rewarding. He turned to the screen next to him.

"Now I'll just call Mr. Savage," he said,

excitement oozing out of his voice. He flipped the screen as it was in the process of connecting, but no face appeared. Instead, a profile icon of a flower filled the screen. Mr. Savage's voice came boomed through the computer – deeply powerful and confident but also seemingly quite young. He spoke with authority and a vague British accent.

"I can't seem to get the picture to work," Mr. Savage said. "Paolo, can you figure this out?" Paolo rapidly punched a few buttons and started to sweat as he fiddled with the computer. Ed and Bo had never seen him like this—afraid, nervous, and kind of unimpressive. Even Paolo was an anxious wreck around his boss.

"No matter, no matter, I can just make the voice work. Hello, Ed and Bo! Welcome to CotLaw, and welcome to your future," Mr. Savage drawled.

"Hi," Bo answered. "Hello," said Ed.

"This is really just a formality, but I wanted to make sure I could meet you before we all become partners. Speaking of which—Paolo, can you stop fiddling with that computer long enough to sign the damn contract?" Paolo shot up straight. He took the contract from his desk.

"Right away, sir." He flipped through it to the last page, and signed with vigor. Just as his pen left the paper, he started to cackle. Mr. Savage quickly shushed him.

"I'm the one who cackles, Paolo," he said, breaking out into an evil cackle.

"Of course sir, I'm so sorry."

Mr. Savage's cackle came through the speakers for a while, and Ed and Bo complacently lounged in their chairs, smiling back at them.

"Well, I think it's time we came clean, my boys," Mr. Savage began. "You've been duped." Mr. Savage burst into more cackles, before stopping abruptly to yell at the competing chuckler.

"Paolo, for the last time, I'm the only one who cackles!" He said angrily. Paolo shook his head vehemently. "It's not me, sir!"

Ed and Bo sat in their chairs, watching the

mess unfold before them and cackling themselves. Cackling is infectious, but Ed and Bo also had their own reason to cackle.

"No, *my* boys," Ed started.

"You've been duped," Bo finished. They sat back and cackled, echoes filling up the entire room and reverberating back to them. After a few glorious moments, Ed and Bo discreetly high-fived each other.

"That was amazing, dude," Ed whispered.

"We totally nailed that," Bo whispered back.

Paolo paled even more and Mr. Savage's voice shot up a few degrees, making him sound like a young boy.

"Paolo? What do they mean?"

"I'm not sure, sir."

Ed smiled and pulled out the original contract from behind his back. "You might want to read what you just signed."

Paolo started to page through the decoy contract on his desk, slowly at first, and then more quickly.

"Oh god, no! Oh no . . . " Paolo murmured, his head in his hands.

"What does it say, Paolo!" Mr. Savage demanded.

But Paolo just shook his head, unable to get out any words. Ed turned to Bo.

"I think we can fill him in?" Ed offered.

"Oh yes. Let's see—most of the clauses are about how Paolo is a stupid idiot who likes to eat his own poop," Bo began.

"And the other clauses are about how CotLaw is full of ugly liars and no one in there can get a date to save their life," Ed added.

"Oh, and the three clauses about Mr. Savage's dick," Bo leaned into the computer. "It's very small." Bo cackled some more.

"Also how Ed and Bo are smart and amazing and—oh yeah, that one last part," Ed said.

"Always read the contract," Bo said with finality. They stood up, both pretty proud of themselves.

"Well, it's been great to 'work' with you," Ed

said as they started to turn away. "But we never want to do it again."

Mr. Savage started to yell after them vague threats about how they'll regret this one day—but Ed and Bo didn't hear. They could only hear Paolo's sobs and the sound of their victory as they walked into the elevator to leave CotLaw for the last time.

11

"**S**o, anyways, that's how the Mona Lisa was actually the very first selfie of all time," Bo concluded. He was sitting in the seat in which he felt most comfortable—that same dilapidated thrift store couch that was molded to the intricacies of his butt.

"You're so full of shit," Ed retorted. He took another hit for emphasis. "There is no way that woman could sit there *and* paint at the same time. You can barely read while you poop."

"I can read texts, thank you very much," Bo responded. "Just like, give me the evidence that someone else painted it, that's all I'm asking."

Ed laughed and passed the DinoBong to Bo.

"There's so much evidence! Literally, all there is is evidence!"

"Then what's the name of whoever 'painted' it?" Bo asked.

"Um . . . it's . . . something French . . . " Ed trailed off, looking down as he realized he didn't exactly know.

"I'll tell you who painted it. Mona Lisa," he declared, expelling smoke in a cool ring pattern. Ed just sat back and laughed. They relaxed in the same smoke-filled garage, relieved to be back in normalcy and away from the lies of CotLaw for good, although still rattled from the whole experience.

"Hey, Ed?" Bo asked.

"Yeah, Bo?"

"Do you think we made the right decision?"

Ed peered over at Bo in surprise. "Of course we did! They were going to take our company and leave us with a measly ten thousand dollars!"

Bo shrugged. "But their work environment is

so cool. Remember how much peanut butter they had? And what if we don't ever make more than ten thousand dollars?" He asked tentatively. Ed began to pack another bowl as he formulated his response.

"Look, even if they were super cool, we want to be cool on our own terms," Ed stated, "not anybody else's. Maybe one day Square One can be like that too, but until then, I think we should just be glad that we learned something."

"Never trust beautiful people?" Bo asked. Ed chuckled.

"Well, yes, that too. But also, always read the contract," Ed said. Bo nodded, taking the bowl from Ed and ready to smoke the evening away. But before they could smoke away even part of the afternoon, Natalie burst into the garage clad in a floor-length purple dress that made her look like an Egyptian queen. Ed and Bo were both immediately taken aback, albeit for different reasons.

"Come on you idiots, it's time for Summer Slam."

Ed and Bo did the only thing they could do in a situation like this: they laughed.

"Natalie, do you think we wouldn't know if tonight was Summer Slam?" Ed said teasingly.

"Yeah, what, like we would just get so wrapped up in our other stuff that we wouldn't even realize that it was time for . . . Summer Slam . . . " Bo trailed off as he looked at Ed in fear.

"Shit, dude," was all Ed could reply. Natalie tapped her heeled toe impatiently and gestured to her watch.

"Let's goooooo weirdoooooos," she drawled impatiently. Bo set down the bong, which was a rare occurrence indeed. Ed wiped his glasses nervously.

"We don't even have any dates!" Ed cried.

"Or anything to wear," Bo added, gesturing to their eternally dirty clothing. Natalie rolled her eyes dramatically.

"You're telling me that at the end of your last

year, you're *not* going to go to the biggest dance in all of Portland?" Ed looked at her skeptically. "The biggest dance in most of our Western Suburban area?" She amended. Ed and Bo both shook their heads defiantly, yet somehow, thirty minutes later they had ended up in Ed's Dad's old closet, searching through formal wear.

"Hurry up!" Natalie shouted from the bedroom. Ed and Bo held up various dress shirts and ties and pants combinations, trying to find the thing that looked cool vintage and not smelly vintage.

"Man, good thing your Dad left all these clothes here," Bo said as he held up a bowling shirt and Ed shook his head. "I mean, not good that he left. But good that we now have these clothes to wear because we forgot to rent tuxes. Know what I mean?" He continued to dig through the piles and piles of old stuff buried in the closet. "Dude. Why does your family have so much map shit everywhere?"

"They used to be into sailing and these long trips," Ed said quietly, because it was kind of a sore subject. Soon he found the treasure he had been looking for: a white tuxedo buried under some old tennis shoes. Bo nodded emphatically. Ed threw his clothes off and pulled on the old tuxedo, which fit his thin build perfectly. Bo nodded in approval.

"At least now I have something from him besides bad vision," Ed offered, marveling at how he looked kind of like a magician. Bo pulled out a pale blue tuxedo, equipped with a ruffled under-shirt. He looked at Ed questioningly and Ed gave him a resounding "thumbs up." Bo struggled to fit the pants on and could just barely button the suit jacket—it was all several sizes too small for a vaguely muscular boy like Bo—and finally sort of finished. He looked like a giant who had tried too hard to put clothes on and might break them at any moment, but the color perfectly comple-mented his slightly tanned skin. Ed gave another "thumbs up" of approval.

"I think I might be a bit too big for this," Bo mumbled, trying to bend over and only reaching a quarter of the way. Natalie barged in and burst out laughing when she saw Bo. He immediately turned bright red and started to take the jacket off, but Natalie stopped him as she chuckled.

"No, come on, I was just surprised is all. You look . . . interesting!" She tried to salvage it, but Bo turned redder and redder.

"I am not showing up like this with no date and a suit that barely fits," Bo mumbled through clenched teeth. Natalie threw up her hands in exasperation.

"Fine! I'll be your date! Let's go!" She started to drag Bo out of the room and he could only look at Ed with a strange mixture of confusion and pure happiness.

"What about Cameron?" Bo asked faintly.

"It's complicated," Natalie said in a tone that suggested she did not want to talk about it. Ed followed them, partially thinking about who Hayley would be going to Summer Slam with and also noticing how Bo seemed to jump whenever Natalie got anywhere near him. When the boys walked out and saw a limo waiting outside, they both immediately felt a flood of panic rising up.

"No, Natalie, don't get in that!" Bo yelled as she neared it.

"They're after us!" Ed added, shrinking back in fear. Natalie rolled her eyes and opened the car door to reveal a non-leather interior and a nice driver who was sporting a cowboy hat.

"Howdy, y'all! Who is ready for a bone-pickin' good time?" The driver shouted out.

"You guys really need to smoke less. Also where did this limo come from?" Natalie asked.

"And what does bone-pickin' mean?" Bo asked.

"Happy last Summer Slam," Ms. DeLancey announced behind them. She was decked out in a globe-covered vest and standing at the doorway, smiling proudly at her kids and her adopted kid.

"I just wanted to get you guys something nice. You should drive in style," she said. For the next twenty minutes, Ms. DeLancey made them pose in various different positions as she took pictures, but such was the price they paid for such a dope ride. After they satisfied her picture requirements, Ed, Bo, and Natalie piled into the limo, smiling giddily. Ed and Bo sat next to each other, as they were used to doing in limos, and Natalie stared back at them.

"You guys look older," she announced, after studying them for a while. "Maybe it's the whole graduation thing, but probably it's just that you need to shave," she said more directly to Ed.

"Natalie, you need to get more friends. Stop hanging out with us, we don't need you at all," Ed responded.

"Yes, you very literally do, because otherwise you wouldn't even know the Summer Slam was today. And also Bo needs me because I'm his date." She smiled at Bo, who nodded in agreement.

"What she said," he announced. Ed shot him a dirty look, but Bo just shrugged in response. "She's my date, man."

Ed shook his head and looked down at his hands. "Alright. Well, you better be a good date, Natalie," he said, and then mouthed loudly to Bo, "I hope you get lucky!"

Bo and Natalie both turned bright red.

"Shut up," Bo snapped a bit too forcefully. Ed did indeed shut up, still curious about the fact that this time, Natalie reddened as well. They rode in silence all the way to the Summer Slam, each trying to look less red before they saw the public.

The limo pulled up to a wide open-air pavilion, ornamented with white stringed lights. "Summer Slam," was spelled out in bright lights and underneath was written "Congratulations to the Interius Montgomery Senior Class." Ed, Bo, and Natalie stood in front of the pavilion as sounds of Top 40 hits, yells from their peers, and clumsy dancing echoed out. The sickly sweet smell of fake chocolate wafted out with the yells, and Ed and Bo both remembered chocolate fondue. They usually spent Summer Slams in the back eating all the food, but perhaps this Slam would be different. They all looked at each other and Bo held out his arm to Natalie. She smiled, put her arm on his, and they walked in.

As soon as Ed and Bo neared the dance floor and started to make a beeline for the fondue pot, people started to notice them. Shy Tenth Grader—they really needed to learn her name—turned and saw them and yelled, "It's Ed and Bo!" The group of students turned around and started to applaud and cheer for them. It was an experience that Ed and Bo only thought happened in movies, so it was jarring to experience it in person. Natalie clapped as well and made eye contact with Bo. She mouthed a simple, "Congratulations." Ed and Bo smiled and thanked people as they kept coming up and saying vague things about their future success. After the fifth or sixth person that came up to them, Ed and Bo made a simultaneous escape to the fondue pot corner.

"Dude. What are they congratulating us for?" Ed asked.

"I was going to ask you that!" Bo responded. "Maybe they think we made that deal . . . ?"

"Nah, they can't have heard about that. Maybe they think we're going to college?" Ed offered.

"I actually meant to talk to you about that," Bo began.

"Yeah, me too," Ed responded tentatively.

Bo took in a deep breath and then breathed out slowly. "I got a move-in email from the University of Washington and I'm not exactly sure why."

"Shit! Me too!" Ed yelled. "When did we apply?"

"When did we get in?" Bo responded. They spent quite a few minutes trying to piece together their college success story but couldn't really get past the fact that they were supposed to move into school the following week. They ended up just deciding that they probably had applied at some point and forgotten about it, as they are prone to do. They also downed between five and thirty-two marshmallows doused in chocolate in the process, because figuring out school was stressful. Meanwhile, the dancing raged on without them. Bo would look over every so often to find Natalie breaking it down near the front, by the DJ, and Ed would look over every so often and see the ever-radiant Hayley leaning in the corner, talking to a friend. The boys stuck to where they were comfortable, the very back of the room.

But, when Cameron Walcot got on the stage and summoned Ed and Bo personally, they didn't exactly have a choice anymore.

"Let's get a speech from the newest business star graduates of I.M. High!" Cameron shouted into the microphone. Cheers ricocheted through the crowd, and Ed and Bo were cheered up to the stage. They begrudgingly made their way through the crowd and up to Cameron, waving and high-fiving a few people along the way. They reached the stage and looked out at their peers before them. Their former peers smiled up at them and genuinely looked please to see them. Ed took the microphone and looked out at the crowd and shrugged. He handed the microphone to Bo, who muttered,

"Thanks," into it, accompanied also with a shrug. They stood there uncomfortably for a few more moments before turning and making their way off stage. Cameron snatched the mic back quickly as the boys walked off. The crowd clapped politely, mostly just confused.

"Thank you, Ed and Bo, for that rousing speech," he said, eliciting laughter from the dancing teens before him. "Now, let's throw it on back to the DJ."

An hour or so later, Ed and Bo had been able to remain in their fondue fortress without any further infringement. Whenever people came to get some fondue, Ed and Bo both turned their heads to hide their faces. It was pretty bizarre, but the class just figured they were shy. In reality, Ed and Bo were shy, and they also were still not exactly sure what they were supposed to be celebrating. They talked about moving into college and the future of Square

One and also Velocidactyls in the corner for most of the evening, hoping to be able to escape before the slow songs. But when that power ballad came on and boys and girls paired from across the room, they knew they were in a dire position. Bo watched as Cameron approached Natalie and she said something with a few accompanying hand motions. He said something back, and she turned around and walked away. Cameron stared after her. Natalie sauntered over to Bo, a little bit drunk from a flask of some sort of liquor stolen from someone's parent, and grabbed him forcibly.

"Come on. You're my date."

Bo shook his head in fear, but Natalie insisted and dragged him over the floor. He shot a scared look back at Ed, who could only stress-eat another marshmallow fondue creation. Bo didn't really have any idea where to put his hands or what to look at or what to look like, so he kind of settled his hands somewhere on Natalie's waist area. Natalie's breath smelled like a hint of whiskey. Even though the smell usually repulsed Bo, it kind of enchanted him on Natalie. They awkwardly swayed around the room in the throngs of all the other awkward swayers, and Natalie leaned in close.

"What do you think you're gonna do now?" she asked.

"Um—like tonight? Or in general?"

"Both."

"I don't know," he said with a laugh. She nodded and spun him around aggressively. As they spun he saw Hayley across the room dancing closely with someone who looked a lot like Danielle. "Is that—" he began, gesturing over to the pair.

"Yep."

"And Danielle—"

"Uh huh."

"Oh," Bo said, and then as it dawned on him, he said it with more meaning. "Oh. So they're . . . "

"Together," Natalie finished abruptly, as if she was daring him to comment on it.

"Does your brother know?"

"Dude. The whole school knows. It was *the* gossip back in May."

"Man. He's an idiot."

Natalie threw her head back and laughed appreciatively. "That's what he gets for treating her like an object and not a person." Bo nodded, a bit awed at the way they were talking so close to each other. "I'm gonna be the president of the Young Feminists' Club next year," she said proudly.

"That's great," Bo said, not exactly knowing what else to say. Natalie took out the flask and offered it to Bo, who took a big gulp and swallowed it in its entirety. He needed courage.

"Thanks," he gasped when he could breath again. She chuckled and took the flask back, but not before taking a swig herself.

"Don't mention it." She leaned in even closer to Bo, making his heart and other parts of his body race with feeling. The liquor made its way through his veins and he felt like he could maybe even dare to do something.

"Seriously. What are you idiots going to do now that you're famous idiots?" She asked with a smile spreading through her eyes. Bo was briefly brought out of his rush of feeling by a touch of confusion.

"What do you mean?" They were spinning faster now, and Bo was starting to feel a bit dizzy and pretty disoriented.

"Come on," she said, looking at him with disbelief. Bo just looked back with blank eyes. "Oh my god," she continued. "You really don't know. I thought you were just pulling the whole modest thing this whole time! You guys don't get out much, do you?" She broke out of the embrace and took Bo by the hand, marching him back over to the fondue fortress, manned by Ed.

"You guys are both idiots and you're both going to be rich," she announced. "I'm so glad I'm the one who gets to tell you. Go on, sit down," she gestured to the seat next to Ed. "You'll want to."

Bo sat down, shrugging at Ed's questioning look.

"I'll be right back," Natalie said as she ran across the room. Bo shook his head as he watched her go.

"I have no idea, man, I was just dancing and minding my own business when she completely flipped out," Bo explained. Ed shrugged, unfazed and a bit depressed.

"I asked Hayley to dance and she told me she likes women," Ed said flatly.

"Bummer, man."

"But also that's not the reason she didn't want to dance with me," Ed continued.

"That's what I've been saying this whole time!" Bo exclaimed.

"Dude! Not the time to rub it in," Ed said dejectedly.

"Right. Sorry. That sucks, dude."

"It's okay. You danced for the both of us, I guess," Ed said, and Bo couldn't exactly place his tone. Before long, Natalie had rushed back, bearing with her a copy of *Business Week*. She threw it down on the table in front of them.

"Natalie, seriously, we didn't come here to read—" but Ed's complaints were cut short when he glanced down at the magazine and saw a picture of himself with Bo on the cover. Bo gaped in amazement. The title: "The Next Big Innovators." They flipped madly to the centerfold, finding a lengthy feature on them and Square One. Ed and Bo both tried to skim as fast as they could, but were only getting every other word.

"Yeah, it basically just talks about how amazing you two are and how you're geniuses with a different kind of work ethic and blah, blah. Nothing too crazy, it just sounds like this chick really liked you guys," Natalie said. Ed turned back to the first page of the story and saw the author's name: Rosalie Müllers.

"She even writes about how she was doing secret research for that company that tried to buy you out but then decided to tell the world about you guys instead. Or something like that," Natalie concluded with a grin. "Anyways, welcome to adulthood, boys. What are you going to do next?"

Ed looked at Bo and Bo looked at Ed, both of them still reeling.

"Um," Ed said.

"Uhhh," Bo trailed off. Natalie sighed and rolled her eyes. "You're going to dance, first and foremost. Then you'll figure out the rest." She pulled them both up, ignoring their protests, and led them to the middle of the dance floor. Ed and Bo started slow but eventually warmed up. A few songs later, Ed was trying to robot, Bo was pretending he could do the worm, and Natalie was cackling at their idiocy. They danced like it was the last night they could be kids, because maybe it was.